A Bunch of Wild Flowers

Book Three

The Wild Flower Trilogy

PAUL HAYWARD

Published by

MELROSE BOOKS

An Imprint of Melrose Press Limited
St Thomas Place, Ely
Cambridgeshire
CB7 4GG, UK
www.melrosebooks.com

FIRST EDITION

Cover design, starcharts and internal illustrations
by Bryan Carpenter

ISBN 1 905226 17 9

Printed and bound in Great Britain by:
Bath Press Limited, Lower Bristol Road,
Bath, BA2 3BL, UK

Contents

Illustrations

BALLAD OF AGINCOURT

One wore his mistress' garter, one her glove;
And he a lock of his dear Lady's hair;
And he had colours, whom he did most love;
There was not one but did some favour wear;
And each one took it, on his happy steed,
To make it famous by some knightly deed

Michael Drayton (1563–1631)

Name Index

ABARIS
(Abb-ah-riss)

In Greek mythology, priest at the temple of god Apollo. As a reward for his services, Apollo gave Abaris a golden arrow to fly through the air. It also made him invisible in flight.

ALBERT ROSS

Enormous white bird. Friend of Dick Tater and Hecate – the Greek mythological goddess of witches.

ANDROMEDA
(Ann-dromm-mid-ah)

Daughter of Queen Cassiopeia. Unpretentious princess. Subsequent wife to Perseus. Unknowingly helped the Greek goddess Athena who, in gratitude, gave Andromeda a ring to seal their friendship (see 'Ring of Friendship'). Athena also immortalised her by placing Andromeda in her own star constellation in the night sky.

ANGELICA

See 'White Archangel'.

APPIAN WAY
*(Also see
 Respighi)*

The courseway used to enter the city of Rome via the Appian Gate. It was called the Appian Way because its construction was first started in 312 BC by the city's censor, Appius Cladius.

ATHENA
(Ath-ee-nah)

Major and powerful goddess. Daughter of Zeus. Also goddess of human maidens. Friend to Andromeda, Flos and later, Poppy and St. John.

ATROPOS
(Att-roe-poss)

One of three goddess sisters (The Fates). She cuts everyone's thread of life when it is time to die.

5

AUNT KAY	Distant relative of Poppy and St. John. She lives in Tevlingorde village, near Honeypot Hill. Owner of 'Pig'. Self-employed chartered accountant. Single, early 30's, slim, shoulder length fair hair, blue eyes.
AURIGA *(Orr-ree-gah)*	Star constellation. Auriga was the Latin word for a charioteer in the Roman gladiatorial circus.
AURORA *(Orr-roar-rah)*	In Roman myth, goddess of the dawn light. *Boreas was god of the North Wind. The Aurora Borealis (Northern Lights) is derived from combining the names of both gods.
BALIUS *(Bay-lee-uss)*	Second lead horse for Auriga's chariot team. Stable-mate to Xanthus
BATTLE OF AGINCOURT	Took place outside the village of Agincourt, France, on 25th October 1415 A.D. King Henry V of England (outnumbered 5 to 1) defeated the French army by clever use of the surrounding terrain, wooden-stake defences and tactical use of his longbow archers.
BRYONY	See 'White Archangel'.
CASSIUS *(Kass-ee-uss)*	Roman soldier. Husband to Flos the 'Flower Girl'. Great ancestor to Poppy and St. John.
CLOTHO *(Kloth-oh)*	One of three goddess sisters (The Fates). She spun everyone's thread of life from birth to death.
COMETS	Frozen balls of ice and rock. Heated up by the Sun, the ice turns to steam and streams back in a tail.
CONSTELLATION	Groups of stars that form patterns in our sky. Often named after the gods/goddesses that live there.
DICK TATER	Nasty northern king. Friend to Albert Ross and Hecate, the Greek mythological goddess of witches.
DRYADS *(Drie-adds)*	'Nymphs of the forests'. Nymphs were believed to be beautiful miniature maiden goddesses with a sprinkle of magic in them. All nymphs were believed to be immortal. However, Dryads lived within trees and when the tree died, the Dryad died with it

ELECTRA *(Ell-eck-trah)*	One of seven goddess sisters living in the Pleiades constellation, which has seven stars in its pattern.
FATES (The)	General term for the three goddess sisters Clotho, Lachesis and Atropos
FLOS *(Fl-oss)*	Slight build, long black hair, pale complexion, heart-shaped face and soft brown eyes. Andromeda's street-urchin friend. 'Flower Girl'. Later, wife to Cassius. Great ancestor to Poppy and St. John
FRAN *(Francesca)* *(Fran-chess-kah)*	Daughter to John Travis. Teenage twin sister to Tony. Round face, dark eyes and full lips. Raven hair, cascading in ringlets to small of her back. Olive complexion betraying origin of her mother's Mediterranean roots.
FRANCESCA da RIMINI	Girl featured in an Italian love-legend. Giovanni Malatesta of the Italian town of Rimini, nicknamed 'Scianciato' (the lame), obtained Francesca in a callous business deal from her father, Guido da Polenta, who was lord of the town of Ravenna. Giovanni sent his younger brother, Poalo, to fetch the girl from Ravenna. During the journey home and with the passing of time, Poalo and Francesca fell deeply in love. In the year 1285 AD, suspecting betrayal, Giovanni stabbed them to death after he had caught them embracing.
GALATEA *(Gal-att-ee-ah)*	See Pygmalion.
GOLDEN ARROW	See 'Abaris'.
GOLDEN BLUEBELL	Magical flower planted by Mother Nature to control all her wild flowers and the four seasons of the year.
GORGONS *(Gore-gone-s)*	Collective name for three sisters – Euryale, Stheno and Medusa. Monsters, so ugly, they turned their victims to stone.
GREAT ONE	Divine Being, who all the gods and goddesses acknowledged to be the supreme power in the universe. To mankind, known as Allah, Buddha, God and so on.

HECATE *(Heck-att-ee)*	In Greek mythology, goddess of witches. Friend to the Gorgon sisters.
HERA *(Here-rah)*	In Greek mythology, the Queen of the Gods and wife to Zeus. Goddess of marriage and childbirth.
HONEYPOT HILL	Wooded hill near Tevlingorde village where the goddess Mother Nature planted the magic Golden Bluebell.
HYDRA *(High-drah)*	In Greek mythology, monster with one hundred heads. The fangs of each mouth delivered a deadly poison. Almost indestructible because as each head was cut off, two more immediately grew in its place. The only way to prevent that happening was to seal the severed neck with fire.
JOHN TRAVIS	Father to Fran and Tony. Government advisor to overseas development department. Experienced light aircraft pilot and engineer. Early forties, square features, fair hair, smiling blue eyes, average height and medium build.
KING HENRY V	See 'Battle of Agincourt'.
LACHESIS *(Lack-ee-siss)*	One of three goddess sisters (The Fates). She chooses events that occur on each person's thread of life.
LARES *(Larr-reeze)*	In Roman mythology the Lares were guardian spirits of the household and family life. At Roman family meals, a food portion was offered to 'their' Lares. A Lares, in Andromeda's heavenly constellation palace, supervised the kitchens that fed all the 'Little Stars'. This Lares befriended Poppy and St. John.
LITTLE STARS	All the children whose lives on Earth were cut short by war and starvation. Andromeda took them into her heavenly palace to provide a full childhood before they passed out into the stars to be met and cared for by their ancestors.
MEDUSA *(Medd-oo-sah)*	In Greek mythology one of three Gorgon sisters, so ugly, that they turned to stone anyone that looked at them.

MERCURY

Messenger to the gods in Roman Mythology. He had small wings on his silver helmet, small wings sprouting from his ankles and carried a winged rod.

MOTHER NATURE

Goddess of all flora and creator of wild flowers. Sent by Zeus to create the beauty of the Earth.

NELSON
Battle of Trafalgar

On the 21st of October 1805, England's 'wooden walls' went into battle under the command of Horatio Nelson at Trafalgar. He led the English fleet in his flagship, H.M.S. Victory. Her English Oak timbers carried 152 cannons and 850 men. Despite being heavily outnumbered by a combined French and Spanish fleet, Nelson drove his ship into the foe and engaged several enemy vessels at once. The enemy was ripped to ribbons and England won a decisive sea victory. Nelson was killed by a sniper's bullet during close engagement.

ORION
(Orr-rye-onn)

In Greek mythology, Orion was a giant and a hunter. His father was Poseidon, god of the seas and brother to Zeus. The line of three stars in his constellation represents the belt around his waist.

PAN

Greek mythological god of fields, hills and woods. A prankster who would leap up and scare travellers that disturbed his slumbers. Our modern word 'panic' derives from the Greek word 'panikos' – of the god Pan – who had a reputation for causing fear and fright.

PEGASUS
(Pegg-ah-suss)

Divine winged horse. Also a star constellation.

PERSEUS
(Perr-see-uss)

Warrior-king of Mycenae. Betrothed to Princess Andromeda. Cut off the head of Medusa and used it to destroy the monster that was going to eat Andromeda.

PIG

Black Ladbrador dog owned by Aunt Kay. Brave, pig-headed, a pig for food and incorrigible rogue.

PLUTARCH
(Ploo-tark)

Born in Greece circa 50 AD. Was a philosopher and a writer. He wrote an historical account of the ancient people of Sparta – the Spartans

POLARIS
(Poe-larr-iss)

The North Pole star. Situated directly above the Earth's axis, it does not appear to move at all.

POPPY

Teenage heroine and twin to her brother St. John. Descendant of Flos 'The Flower Girl'. Slight build, long black hair, pale complexion, heart-shaped face and soft brown eyes. Named by her mum after the Poppy flower.

PROFESSOR POULTNEY

Retired astronomer. Lives in Tevlingorde village. Friend of Aunt Kay. Befriends Poppy and St. John.

PYGMALION
(Pigg-may-lee-on)

In Roman mythology, a sculptor who carved statue of a beautiful woman from block of stone. Named her Galatea and fell in love with her. In answer to his prayers, Venus, goddess of love, endowed statue with life and Galatea became Pygmalion's wife.

RESPIGHI
Ottorino
(Ress-pee-gy)
b.1879 – 1936
(Also see
Appian Way)

Composer. Wrote the music 'Pines of Rome'. The 4th movement is entitled 'Pines of the Appian Way' and is designed to invoke in the listener's mind the ancient triumphal march of the victorious legions as they entered Rome and home! You can order and borrow the CD from your local library. Close your eyes and let the music transport you back in history. See the glint of the the gold eagles atop the swaying legion's standards and shimmer of silver and gold red plumed helmets in the sun as they emerge from the morning mist. Hear the clatter of horses hooves, the rumbling of chariot wheels on the paved Appian Way and the roars of the flower-throwing welcoming crowds. Or imagine Poppy and St. John making their own triumphal parade before their army.

RING OF FRIENDSHIP

Andromeda unknowingly helped the Greek goddess Athena who, in gratitude, gave her a ring to seal their friendship. It became known among the gods as 'Andromeda's Ring of Friendship'. Flos, in turn, saved the life of Andromeda and she gave it to Flos at a ceremony dedicated to 'Friendship'. Flos bequeathed it to her daughter and through the female generations, it came to be worn by Poppy – a descendant of Flos.

ROSE FLOS

Descendant of Flos the 'Flower Girl'. Mother of the twins Poppy and St. John.

SORREL

See 'White Archangel'.

ST. JOHN
(Sin-junn)

Teenage hero and twin to his sister Poppy. Descendant of Flos 'The Flower Girl' and Cassius. Stocky build, angular features, blue eyes and tousled fair hair. Named by his mother after the St. John's Wort wild flower.

STHENO
(Stee-noe)

One of three Gorgon sisters, monsters so ugly that, to look upon them turned the victim to stone.

TONY

Son to John Travis. Teenage twin brother to Fran. Square features, short fair hair, smiling blue eyes but studious furrow to his brow. Average height and medium build.

VIOLETTA

Golden Labrador bitch transformed by Poppy from a Dog Violet wild flower. Girlfriend to Pig.

WHITE ARCHANGEL

Common British wild flower appointed by Mother Nature as 'guardians' over her wild flower creations. When destruction threatened all wild flowers, the White Archangel flowers transformed into angels named Angelica, Bryony and Sorrel. They set out to enlist the help of Poppy and St. John.

XANTHUS
(Zann-tuss)

First lead-horse for Auriga's chariot team. Given the power of speech by Hera (Queen of the gods) to warn Achilles at the siege of Troy that he was vulnerable to pending death.

YEW TREE

The wood is very strong and resilient. Used to make the famed English longbow. Held to be a decisive weapon in the English victory at the Battle of Agincourt.

ZEPHYR
(Zeff-err)

Greek mythological god of the West Wind and father of the immortal horses Xanthus and Balius.

ZEUS
(Zee-oos)

In Greek mythology, the King of the Gods in the heavens. Husband to Hera, father to Athena.

Introduction

To those it may concern:

"**Flowers of the Gods**", which was Book One of *The Wild Flower Trilogy*, started at the beginning of time when Earth was made beautiful by the goddess Mother Nature who planted wild flowers across its surface. She then placed a golden Bluebell on a wooded hill in the middle of England. The Bluebell's divine power held total control over the four seasons of the year and her wild flowers all over the world.

It also told how the gods and goddesses of Greek and Roman mythology played a part in making that happen. However, the selfish actions of some of the gods at that time were about to destroy every wild flower and the world we live in today.

Ancient history shows that there were many gods and goddesses in Greek and Roman times. There were also giants and monsters. Some later dwelt on Earth but most lived in the heavens in constellations.

Constellations are groups of stars that form patterns in our night sky. Each constellation has its own name. Usually, the star pattern is named after the god, goddess, monster, or animal that lives in that constellation. They can all be seen with the naked eye on a clear night. To help pick them out, star maps of our night sky were included in Book One.

"**Children of the Stars**", which is Book Two of *The Wild Flower Trilogy*, also contained maps of our night sky. These were useful to follow Poppy Hayward and her twin brother, St. John Hayward, on their travels through the stars. Due to the squabbles of the gods in the distant past, the teenagers' mundane lives were thrown into chaos when they were sent right across the heavens in a dangerous quest to find a way of saving every wild flower on Earth. In fact, to save the very Earth itself!

"**A Bunch of Wild Flowers**", which is Book Three of *The Wild Flower Trilogy*, includes illustrations of the common British wild flowers that feature in this concluding book. The sketches will be useful to spot the featured plants while walking in the countryside. Do not look too closely though – just in case you find the Golden Bluebell that was planted by the goddess, Mother Nature. No one could be trusted with the power it holds if they got their hands on it!

Additionally, the pictures will be useful for identification purposes as each wild flower makes its appearance in the culmination to the trilogy. When Poppy and St. John return to Earth from their dangerous journey through the stars, they alone have to face the greatest evil ever known to mankind. The only source they can turn to for help is "A Bunch of Wild Flowers".

The story now picks up as Poppy and St. John are about to re-enter the Earth's atmosphere.

CHAPTER 1
THE TRAVIS TALE

St. John carefully aligned the Golden Arrow of Abaris over the imaginary line of the Earth's polar axis and then plunged down along its path from the star of Polaris towards the planet's North Pole. Within seconds he was frantically gripping the violently shuddering shaft, desperate to keep control as the arrowhead kicked wildly from the resistance caused by ripping through the atmosphere. The friction from their re-entry exploded into a searing heat that erupted around them in a roaring fireball. Their reduction to charcoaled lumps of melting flesh and dripping fat was imminent. Poppy screwed her eyes shut, clamped her teeth and waited for inevitable death. However, Athena's electric-blue protective shield held firm for them. In a state of almost fear-crazed gibbering, Poppy uttered aloud her gratitude to the goddess for her help.

As they slowed and drew closer to the lower reaches of the atmosphere, the scream of the fireball and the licking of the flames subsided. The blessed relief to their shredded nerves was short-lived. It was destroyed by the next thought that invaded their tired minds: "We've been through so much, yet the worst is still to come!"

At the same moment as St. John and Poppy were sliding onto the Earth's polar axis, John Travis was sliding into the pilot's seat of his light aircraft at Manchester Airport. He was a fair-haired man of average height, medium build, smiling blue eyes and in his early forties. Flying was in his blood – he loved it. He also deeply appreciated the engineering skills that had gone into every nut and bolt of his aircraft's design. His grandfather had been a Lancaster bomber pilot in the Second World War and had been awarded the DSO and DFC, while John's father had later become a design engineer. Both had spent their life starting up and establishing their own company building light aircraft. As a result, John had learned to fly at an early age. After his grandfather died, John's dad managed the day to day running of the company and John frequently travelled abroad getting orders for their planes. From that, John Travis had made a lot of political contacts within various governments in Eastern Europe, the Middle East, Asia and Africa. He had also gained a wealth of knowledge about international protocol.

It was while in Rome that he had met and married his wife and brought her home to England. At first, they lived with his mother and father at their large farmhouse in southern Leicestershire. It had lovely gardens, an extensive cobbled yard, stable block, numerous brick outbuildings, acres of land and a wooded hill. Initially, it was helpful to John's newly-wed wife to be at the farmhouse. It helped her settle down to a new life in a strange country – particularly as John was away quite a bit at that time. Eventually, the couple bought their own home at Lutterworth, a small market town nearby and not far from the aircraft factory.

It was quite fitting that they should live at Lutterworth because that was where Frank Whittle had started his work on inventing the first jet engine prior to the beginning of the Second World War. Recently, with private donations, a monument had finally been erected to commemorate Whittle's world-changing achievement. It was a life-sized replica of the Gloster E.28/39 aircraft (sometimes known as the Pioneer) which was specially designed to have the new jet engine fitted to it. The plane stands on a traffic island at Lutterworth, just off junction 20 of the M1, and acted as a 'welcome home' sign for John each time he drove back from London.

Shortly after John and his wife got their own house at Lutterworth, she gave birth to twins. The boy, as stated on the birth certificate, was named Anthony, but to his Italian mum it was always 'Antonio'. To his dad and school friends, who eventually won the day by weight of numbers, it was plain 'Tony'. The girl was named Francesca. Mum had put her foot down on that one and exerted her right as mother to name her own daughter. Mum was a bit of a romantic and gave her daughter the name Francesca from the famous Italian love story of Francesca Da Rimini.

When she was old enough, mum told her daughter the story behind her name. Apparently, a seedy fellow named Giovanni Malatesta from the Italian town of Rimini, who was nicknamed Scianciato (the lame), obtained Francesca in a callous business deal from her father, Guido da Polenta, who was lord of the town of Ravenna. Giovanni sent his younger brother, Poalo, to fetch the girl from Ravenna for his 'unwholesome purposes', which Poalo reluctantly did. During the journey home and with the passing of time, Poalo and Francesca fell deeply in love. In the year 1285 AD, suspecting betrayal, Giovanni stabbed them both to death after he had caught them embracing. Young love had suffered separation in life but had triumphantly united in death. So that is how Francesca got to be named. However, much to her mum's romantic disappointment (and everyone else's disregard for history and legend) she was commonly known to all as just plain 'Fran'.

The Travis's were a happy, tight-knit family. Life was going well until their names were flagged-up for The Fates to carry out an annual review – as was their divine duty in relation to everyone. Clotho, the *Spinner of the Thread of Life*, and Lachesis, who determined the *Lots of Life*, conferred with Atropos, the *Cutter of the Thread*, and she decided it was time to get out her snippers. The first that the family knew of the decision of The Fates, as the three little goddesses were collectively known, was when John's father collapsed at the factory and died from a heart attack. This was shortly followed by the death of John's mother.

Her doctor said it was pneumonia but local villagers diagnosed it as a broken heart. Actually, she was not due to pass on so quickly after the death of her husband and there had been a bit of a tiff over that between The Fates. Clotho and Lachesis had accused Atropos of going soft because she felt sorry for the heartache that the old woman was suffering and cutting her thread of life early.

John had to appoint the best salesman he could find as his replacement while he returned to manage the engineering works. The family coped with their sad loss as well as they could and as the months passed they seemed to be recovering from the blow. Then, along came the third decision of The Fates. It was found that John's wife had terminal cancer. Tony and Fran faced up to their mother's illness bravely enough but their dad could no longer balance the responsibilities and demands of the company against the needs of his wife and children. With a heavy heart, he sold the firm and put his family first. They would be financially secure for now and could concentrate on trying to hold the devastating situation together while looking after mum and each other in what was a protracted affair. Finally, Atropos cut the thread, leaving just Tony, Fran and their dad. After what they had been through, any spark of interest in the world around them had gone. They were bereft of any meaning to life. Whatever small thought they had ever given to the abstract concepts that touched on the divine, or how they fitted into the universe, faded away – just as their mother had done.

With his international experience and contacts, John took a civil service post as an adviser within the Government's Department of Overseas Aid and Development. He shut out the recent past by burying himself in his work. Tony and Fran withdrew into themselves and automatically went through the motions of their final months at school, home and school again. They avoided talking to each other about what had happened. Each came up with their own personal excuses for doing this, be it fear of rekindling the pain in the other or fear of being thought of as not coping – stiff upper lip and all that. Consequently, none of the important questions that could help them move on ever got discussed, questions such as:

Where were their grandparents and mum now? Is that all there is – do we all just live and die like beetles on a dung heap? Does 'dust to dust, ashes to ashes' mean exactly that? Or was there more to come for mum? Was there more to come for them?

CHAPTER 2
HOOK, LINE AND SINKER

As John slid into the pilot's seat, his love of flying made him feel positive again. He had flown himself up to Manchester to deliver a speech at an overseas investment lunch and had decided to take his teenage children with him for the ride. John turned and gave Fran and Tony a smile, which they were glad to return because they had not seen him smile in a long time. He studied them fondly for a moment. Fran had a round face, dark eyes and full lips. Her raven hair, of which she was very proud, cascaded in ringlets to the small of her back. Fran was the reflection of her mum and her olive complexion betrayed the origin of her mother's Mediterranean roots. Tony had taken after his dad. He had square features, short fair hair and smiling blue eyes that balanced the studious furrow on his brow. He, too, was of average height and medium build.

John turned back to his aircraft controls and as he adjusted them for take-off his positive feelings gave him the courage to make a decision he had long put off. He decided that when they got home he would face up to returning to his parent's home, going through their personal things and putting the farmhouse and land up for sale. It was a fine, clear evening and dusk was some way off yet. The plane skimmed down the runway and lifted lazily into the air. Fran and Tony leaned back behind their dad and relaxed, confident in his flying skills. They watched the runway lights of Manchester disappear behind them as dad set a course for East Midlands Airport in Leicestershire and home.

Meanwhile, St. John and Poppy had completed their re-entry into the Earth's atmosphere and the former levelled the Golden Arrow out over the Arctic. Then he guided them across the ice cap to Ellesmere Island. From there they skimmed the waters of Baffin Bay, down the west coast of Greenland and shot over the water to join the Labrador coast of Canada. It was now an easy task to trace along the Canadian east coast and that of the USA to New York. He hovered around New York's JFK Airport for a while to see if he would be lucky. His luck was in and it was only a short time before he spotted Concorde taking off for its final flight to London before withdrawal from service.

Their invisibility whilst riding the Golden Arrow of Abaris allowed St. John and Poppy to fly close alongside the supersonic jet and look in the windows at the passengers being served an early evening meal without causing them any alarm. The sight brought immediate pangs of hunger to the twins and without being asked, Poppy leaned over St. John's shoulder and thrust a pile of sandwiches and fruit pie in his hand that the Lares had packed for them. "Who needs plastic food," Poppy smilingly thought to herself, "when you can have wholesome roly-poly home cooking straight from the kitchens of Andromeda's palace?" The Concorde showed a clean pair of heels to the odd lumbering jumbo jet and was soon flashing along at Mach 2. St. John kept the Golden Arrow in place above it for a few hundred miles, took a rough directional line from the plane's course, then zipped off ahead and left the Concorde standing.

He picked up Ireland, flew over Dublin and on towards Wales. Picking up Holyhead on Holy Island, he kicked south-west to the Berwyn Mountains. St. John was familiar with that area because in happier times, mum and dad had taken them pony trekking around there. Poppy had a natural knack with horses even then, which was a bit different to St. John who could never get them to do what they were supposed to do. It was always his horse cantering off with a snigger, leaving him hanging from a tree branch. Poppy sarcastically used to tell everyone that they had been pony-trekking, but in her brother's case, *he* had been pony-wrecking! From the Berwyns, it was easy to pick off Oswestry, Shrewsbury and fly to the north of Birmingham. Looking down from the Golden Arrow, the city centre appeared as a sunflower of yellow street lights with the silver petals of the motorways radiating from it. The tiny fireflies, which were actually cars, buzzed up and down them. Over Cannock, St. John pulled the Golden Arrow slightly north-west and headed for East Midlands Airport. That was the last landmark on his list. They would then only be a few miles from Honeypot Hill and Aunt Kay's.

John gained clearance to land from the control tower and started his gentle three degrees descent into East Midlands Airport. Above, Poppy watched the winking red light of the plane's port wing and the green of the starboard wing steadily gliding dead-centre down towards the two lines of glittering runway lights. It made a pretty, peaceful picture. Suddenly, Poppy screamed out in fear: "For God's sake, look out!"

Sitting in the cosy warmth of the cockpit neither John nor his family heard her desperate yell. His first awareness of danger was the bulk of a gigantic white object that ripped across his line of vision. There came the hissing sound of a sharp intake of breath from Tony and Fran, followed by a clanging noise and the grating of metal as the plane's twisted propeller was pushed up in front of the windscreen. John's head banged against the side of the cockpit from the force of the impact. There was a splutter and cough from the engine. The last thing John heard, before he drifted into unconsciousness, was an eerie silence as the engine cut out. The momentary lapse into silence was shattered by the screams of Fran, brought forth by the fear of imminent death. The white bulk that had streaked by the windscreen had long gone. The only thing that remained of it was a three metre long feather that belonged to the giant bird - Albert Ross. He glided on, untouched and unconcerned.

"What the hell hit that?" shouted St. John over his shoulder.

"It's that enormous bird that Electra told us about," replied Poppy. "Remember? The one that Hecate sent halfway across the world to locate the Golden Bluebell. The evil bitch has sent it to finish us off if we ever managed to survive the Hydra. She.........."

St. John cut her short. "Look! The nose is tilting," he exclaimed. "The plane's going down!"

Without thinking, he wrenched the Golden Arrow hard left and put it into a steep dive to level out in front of the nose of the aircraft.

"Turn round Poppy and face the Arrow's feathers," he commanded. "I'm going to hook them under the plane's nose and keep it up. Reverse me in and for our sake do it right or we'll all be mangled," he muttered under his breath.

"You know that when the Arrow makes contact with the plane it will make us visible to those inside don't you?" cautioned Poppy. "Our secret's blown."

"Yes, and we both know we have no choice don't we," retorted St. John. "Otherwise, whoever is in there is going to die."

Poppy swivelled around on the shaft of the Golden Arrow to face the plane. Her arm shot up high and her fingers beckoned St. John in urgently but carefully. The Arrow gave a kick. Contact was made and held firm between them. The plane levelled out and maintained height under the power of the Arrow. However, St. John was struggling to hold course because the plane's wings were tilting from side to side and threatening to slide the nose off the dart's shaft. St. John shouted at Poppy in desperation. "For Christ's sake, get the pilot to hold it level on the horizontal, otherwise I'm going to lose them!"

"I can't," she pleaded helplessly. "The propeller is up against the windscreen of the cockpit. I can't signal to anyone inside because I can't see a thing and the pilot certainly won't be able to see me out here."

"I don't give a damn," St. John snapped back at her. "I've got my own problems. Just do it!"

As he struggled for control, Poppy's eyes, wide with panic and desperation, stared at the mangled nose and propeller. She was at a complete loss as to what to do. Then her eyes narrowed with concentration at the glint of an idea.

Inside the cockpit, Tony and Fran struggled without success to bring their father round. In their frenzy they had not noticed that the plane, although wobbling from side to side, had suddenly taken a level course. Their awareness of this and the reason why was soon brought into sharp focus. A silver blade started to cut through one of the distorted propeller blades. Within seconds, the twisted metal spun away into the twilight. Through the cracked glass of the cockpit, hovering straight in front of Tony's eyes, was a long dagger. The blue sheen from its blade and the glitter from its sapphire-encrusted handle transfixed him. The dagger then whipped around to the next twisted length of propeller and cut through it like a knife through butter. It hovered for second, slowly backed off from the windscreen and then whizzed away in a wide arc.

Tony's eyes followed its reverse journey and his body stiffened in shock as it completed its circuit.....and 'home'! There, sitting on a huge golden arrow, was a girl with long black hair, topped with a crown of flowers. Her white gown was strewn with embroidered poppies and a gold belt and scabbard hung across her shoulder. His first object of fixation, the knife, now nestled its way back into the girl's outstretched hand. The girl instantly became the second object of his fixation. In one graceful movement, without averting her eyes from his, she sheathed Athena's dagger. So Tony knew the truth at last. "Not only do angels exist," he thought, "but you actually see them before you are about to die".

The angel silently mouthed something to him. He strained his eyes to read her lips. "It's a nice mouth," he thought to himself. "And those lips are luscious. If she lives in Heaven, I want to be there. Just some pain to pass through first but she would be worth it." When the penny finally dropped concerning what she was saying, the words jerked Tony back from his fantasy. "Watch me," they said and she pointed a finger at herself. The angel then stretched her arms out wide with the palms of her hands facing up. Keeping her arms straight out, she started to tilt them up and down and then pointed to the plane's control column. Realisation finally dawned on Tony.

"Quick Fran," he ordered. "Help me get dad out of his seat." They pulled him onto the floor and as Fran cradled her father's head, Tony slipped into the seat and nodded his understanding of the angel's gesture.

Fran's hands instinctively nursed her father while her eyes stared at the impossible vision outside. She saw the girl facing them but was more fascinated by the outline of the figure wrestling with the tip of the Arrow. The strong, young male figure was dressed in a white ancient Greek-style tunic, with a bronze shield on his back and a sword at his side. She glimpsed his face a couple times as he turned to anxiously cast a backward glance and check the arrow's trim. His blonde hair matched the yellow flower embroidered on his chest. To Fran, he looked everything she ever thought a legendary god of youth would look like.

Poppy watched the wings of the plane carefully. As its port wing dipped, she would dip her right arm in response. Then she would curl her fingers upward to indicate the need to lift it. Tony gingerly adjusted the controls and as the wing lifted, so the angel's straight right arm would move up with it. When the wing reached the horizontal, the upward-beckoning fingers of her hand would shoot straight out. Tony would then do his best to hold it there - encouraged by her smiling face of approval. "Lord," thought Tony, "she is lovely". Poppy was indeed giving Tony her smiling approval but the smiles were not all directed at his actions; some were for the young man himself. With each deviation off the horizontal, Poppy would carry out the same procedure and Tony would follow her gestures in blind, trusting faith. "What else would you do with an angel?" he mused. All the time, St. John was trimming the Golden Arrow's descent towards the runway and sweating from the effort of constantly adjusting to Tony's flying errors and Poppy's corrections. The runway lights grew brighter and brighter as the concrete rushed up to meet them.

"Hold on Poppy," came his strangled cry. "This is it!"

There was a bang as the plane wheels hit the ground. The plane bounced, rose into the air and thumped onto the concrete again. The Golden Arrow became disconnected and was thrown to the right. Both the Golden Arrow and its riders became invisible again. The aircraft slewed off to the left and came to rest in silence. There was no movement within.

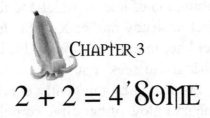

Chapter 3

2 + 2 = 4'80me

Inside the aircraft, Tony sat dazed in the pilot's seat. Fran felt groggy from a bump she had suffered and a tiny smear of blood trickled from a graze on her forehead. The jolt from the landing had roused their father from his unconsciousness and he stirred in her arms. St. John whipped the Golden Arrow around and brought it to a halt next to the aircraft's door. They, and the Golden Arrow, became visible again as both of them jumped off and ran to the door. Poppy wrenched it open and dived in. She reached Tony, cupped his head in her hands and turned his face towards hers. She studied it for a second, looking for any signs of pain in his expression that might signal injury. "It is a nice face," she thought to herself. Then she looked into his eyes to check their alertness and awareness of the situation. She found herself thinking how soft and kind they seemed. There was a slight crinkling of his brow and then the eyes smiled up at her. An overwhelming feeling of tenderness, which she had never experienced before, swept over Poppy. Quickly, she snapped herself out of it. Her effort to pull herself together was spurred more by embarrassment than the gravity of the situation.

"Quick," she prompted, "we've got to get the pilot out."

"Yes. Of course. Dad. How is he?" Tony also had to pull his thoughts back to reality and away from the same feelings of attraction that Poppy had just experienced. Together, they helped his recovering father to his feet and out of the plane. They sat him down on the grass at the side of the runway.

Back in the plane, St. John was tending to Fran. He ascertained that she appeared uninjured and gently helped her to her feet. As she rose, the combination of intense relief and the onset of shock caused Fran to feel unsteady on her feet. St. John put his arms around her and held her to him for support. He looked down into Fran's face enquiringly to seek assurance of her wellbeing. He was immediately fascinated by the gently curving roundness of it, enhanced by the soft glow of her olive complexion. It was the eyes that gripped him, the big, dark eyes that looked up at him. There was a contradictory presence of sensuous dreaminess about them, yet a challenging glint of determined independence. The sum total of those facial nuances radiated an angelic innocence that brought forth in St. John a surge of masculine protectiveness towards her.

It was then that he noticed the graze on her forehead. He brought up his hand to brush away the wisp of hair that obstructed his inspection of the cut but the hand was no longer his any more. It was now a hand that was acting independently, guided by desire. His fingers pushed away the curl but tantalisingly continued over the raven crown and floated down the tumbling cascade of hair to the small of her back. His hand lingered there with ever increasing pressure. She smiled at him and a tell-tale blush came to her cheeks. Their mutual bonding of affection was instantly finished and complete, yet the sweetness of the moment would be everlasting.

The moment was shattered by a shout from Poppy, enquiring if they were alright. Her question suddenly brought the outside world crashing in on their spellbound cocoon like a rockslide. St. John forced himself to snap out of it and hurriedly helped Fran out of the plane. He held her far more tightly than was necessary. There was a wail of sirens and the lights of an ambulance and fire engine in the distance as they raced up the runway. Poppy glanced with alarm at St. John. "We better disappear quickly."

They scurried to the Golden Arrow which was dutifully hovering where they had left it. Their exit was followed by enquiring shouts from Tony and Fran: "Where are you going? Who are you? Where do you come from? Will we see you again?"

The pair straddled the shaft of the Golden Arrow and disappeared into thin air - right in front of the searching eyes of Fran and Tony. With amazement, they heard the voice of St. John come from nowhere.

"Don't worry. We're still here. We'll follow you then talk to you again when you are alone. Please, please, do not mention us to anybody until we get to speak to you and explain."

The emergency services arrived and the survivors were taken back to the rear of the airport terminal where they were escorted to its first aid facilities. Poppy and St. John had followed closely behind the ambulance. They could see Tony and Fran through the rear windows. Each felt a stirring they had not experienced before. St. John's feelings soared even more when he saw Fran's face pressed to the glass and her wide searching eyes straining to peer out into the darkness. His heart pounded a little at the thought that she was looking for him! He could not resist the urge to reach forward and stroke that lovely face through the glass. As his fingertips started to trace along the line of her full red lips, Fran's eyes suddenly became startled and she jerked back in surprise. The contact of St. John's finger with the window of the ambulance had made him visible. She quickly recovered and pressed back to the glass again. This time, her inviting lips were smiling at him and she urgently pressed her hand to the glass so that the outline of it matched the spread of his fingertips.

Fran's brother leaned forward, inquisitive about what she was doing. He caught sight of St. John and then his chest went tight as he glimpsed his own saving angel. Tony's face broke into a slightly lop-sided smile and his eyes radiated a longing for Poppy. Her return smile reflected that longing back to him.

"What are you doing Fran? Are you okay?" her father asked. He was now sitting up and obviously feeling a lot better. St. John yanked his hand off the window and instantly disappeared.

"Nothing dad," she replied breathlessly. Her eyes darted warily to Tony's face, which smirked back in response to the blush on her cheeks.

"No. She's not doing anything dad," said Tony. "After all, there's nothing of interest to see out there. Isn't that right Fran?"

Fran curled her lip and gave him a rebuking glare.

They were ushered into the building by a nurse with two airport officials and guided to a medical care/rest room. The door that the nurse had closed behind them slowly swung wide open again. An official grunted in annoyance, got up and slammed it shut. Poppy and St. John hovered near the ceiling and watched the proceedings below. While the nurse tended to their cuts and bruises, the officials asked the family a few questions. John told them that he had seen a white blur, heard a bang and then knew nothing of what happened after that due to becoming unconscious. Fran and Tony again reiterated their previous statement that they had seen nothing.

"Then what did you see after the initial collision with the white blur?" an official asked the pair. Back came the same negative reply from both.

"Well you must have seen the figures outside the plane," stated one of the men pointedly. "They were smack in front of your noses!"

"What figures?" asked Fran, who was trying to sound as stupid as possible.

Struggling to contain their frustration, the officials explained as patiently as they could that three air traffic controllers had seen what they swore were the outlines of two human figures moving about in front of the plane who somehow seemed to be guiding it down. Both men then glared at Tony. Their silent, questioning stare was demanding a reply. He shuffled uncomfortably, desperately trying to think of a plausible answer, but could not conjure up anything.

"Weeeeell," he replied, his mind frenziedly trying to buy time, "actually, it was....." Fran moved to his side. As she did so, she ground her heel into the top of his foot. His face contorted in pain. Tony tried to disguise his agonised grimace as furrowed concentration.

"Actually," interrupted Fran, still trying to sound cerebrally challenged, "they weren't the outlines of two human figures at all. They were an angel and a Greek god if you must know."

Their father's concerned eyes shot to their faces. Tony returned his look. "Fran got a really bad bump on the head dad when the plane hit the ground." Tony shrugged his shoulders and put a finger to his temple in a screwing motion, as if to indicate she had 'lost it'. He deviously followed this up by stating he thought he had also received a bang on the head and it had made his memory of the whole incident hazy. He put the palm of a hand to his own forehead in affectation. John looked quizzically at the pair of them. He knew his kids well - they were lying through their teeth! However, he had never had cause to distrust them and felt that they must be deliberately acting that way for a very good reason. He allowed his gaze to fall to the floor and said nothing.

The nurse stepped into the conversation and exerted her medical authority. "It's quite clear gentlemen that at least two of these people have had a blow to the head and are suffering concussion, or shock, or both," she said haughtily. "I am going to get the ambulance to take them to the hospital for head x-rays. I suggest you go and stick your little broken aeroplane back together if you want to play detectives and leave my patients alone!"

The men stormed out of the room. The nurse smiled at Tony and Fran reassuringly. "You poor things," she soothed, "you must be in a right state. Now sit quietly while I go and fetch the driver." As she left the room, Fran and Tony smiled triumphantly at each other.

"Right you two," demanded their dad, "I'm waiting for an explanation."

"Look dad, we don't really understand it ourselves," said Tony hesitantly, "but we'll do our best."

Fran interjected. "Even if we can put it into words, I can't see why you should believe us. Even though we saw everything with our own eyes, we're still having trouble getting to grips with it."

They excitedly explained to their father every detail of the miracle, from the mysterious collision of the plane, to its guiding down and their safe deliverance by the angel and the youthful Greek god, followed by seeing their saviours again afterwards through the ambulance window.

"That's who I was looking at when you asked me what I was doing dad. I couldn't tell you then because the ambulance men would have heard. They, whoever 'they' are, pleaded with us to keep their existence secret. If only they were here now," sighed Fran, "it would make it easier for all of us."

"We are," came St. John's voice from somewhere above them. He floated the Golden Arrow down to floor level and as he and Poppy slid off, they popped into view in front of the incredulous family.

"That's them!" shouted Fran in wonderment. "The Greek god and the angel."

She impetuously rushed forward and flung her arms around St. John's neck. Without thinking, his arms slipped around her waist. Again, he looked longingly down into those big dark eyes. St. John felt a warm flush spreading across his face. He so desperately wanted to kiss her but was aware of the presence of her father and did not feel it was right to blatantly take liberties like that. He dropped his arms and pulled away slightly before his desire got the better of his manners. Fran looked disappointed. Tony held no such inhibitions and strode across to Poppy. "Thanks for saving our lives," he murmured. "I don't know whether you can get struck with a thunderbolt for showing disrespect to an angel but it's worth it." With that, his hands gripped her shoulders, pulled her face towards his and he gave her a big kiss of gratitude on the cheek. Poppy gave a gasp of surprise and Tony quickly turned away, embarrassed at his own involuntary action. She had to re-adjust her crown of wild flowers, which were now on the tilt.

St. John felt he had to say something quickly to break the spell Fran was holding over him before he totally lost control and stole a kiss from her as well. He turned to her father to introduce himself:

"Sir, my name is St. John and I'm no Greek god. This is Poppy. She is my sister and she is certainly no angel!" Poppy glared at him and kicked his ankle for daring to embarrass her like that in front of Tony.

"There, you see," he said in vindication, "I rest my case! We haven't come down from the heavens. Well, that's not quite true. We just have actually but we don't live there. We're just two ordinary young people who live on an inner city estate up north."

"Yes, of course you are," said John cynically, "but ordinary people do not just drop down out of the heavens and have a Golden Arrow that makes them invisible to fly around on. What were you two supposed 'ordinary people' doing up there anyway and how did that fantastic Golden Arrow come to be in your possession?"

Things were now getting a bit complicated. Poppy and St. John sat down to deliberately give the haziest story they could. They explained that they had been sent on a mission (but they did not say what) to obtain certain information and objects from space (but they did not say what) and return to execute certain plans to complete their objective (but they did not say what). During the proceedings, Tony had furtively taken hold of Poppy's hand and continued to hold it, in awe, throughout. In her admiration and emboldened by her brother's action, Fran had taken St. John's hand tightly in hers.

"And that's about it really," said St. John. "We were on the way back, saw your plane in trouble and helped out - that's all."

Fran gave his hand a grateful squeeze and those eyes smiled up at him again. "Oh, please," thought St. John, "I wish she wouldn't look at me like that - it's driving me crazy."

"Just as a matter of interest," said John, with feigned nonchalance, "what was it that hit my plane?"

"It was a gigantic white bird," said Poppy without thinking. She realised that her reply was a mistake. She could see from the doubtful look returning to John's face that their story was losing credibility in his eyes again. In an effort to restore the feasibility of it, Poppy threw in the fact that the bird's name was Albert Ross. That only seemed to exacerbate his doubts.

It was not until the next day, after John had read the newspaper headline '**Giant Three Metre Long Bird's Feather**' and the sub-heading 'Found near East Midlands Airport - Expert from Leicester University Zoology Department baffled!' that he fully realised he had been in the presence of two amazing young people.

"Now then," said Poppy to St. John, but gazing at Tony instead, "we must go. The nurse will be back in a minute and we still have a lot of tasks to do before our mission is finished."

She rose and her brother followed her towards the Golden Arrow. Tony's hand brushed against Poppy's and in a mutual response they snatched a momentary last embrace. St. John cast a quick glance at Fran and wrung his hands together in a turmoil of feelings. His shyness rendered him immobile. She stood there, silently daring him to steal a kiss from her. He turned away in acute embarrassment, climbed on the Golden Arrow and promptly disappeared. In desperation, Fran lunged at the spot where she thought he was. She fell over the Golden Arrow's invisible shaft, totally disappeared as her feet left the floor and then reappeared as she tumbled out on the other side.

Fran sprang up again in cheated annoyance. Gently, her arms started to rise out slightly from her sides, as if increasing pressure was being applied under her armpits. Her feet started to rise onto her tiptoes. St. John and the Golden Arrow briefly appeared as his hands lifted her up. As her feet left the floor, both completely disappeared. There was a very short silence, followed by a very long "mmmmmmmm". Fran suddenly reappeared again. She stood motionless, her head tilted back and her eyes still closed. The sound of footsteps and different male voices to the previous ones came close to the door. St. John put his feet down for the Golden Arrow to appear and Poppy to locate it. She jumped on board out of sight.

"Will I see you again?" shouted Tony after her.

"Yes. Yes, I really want to," Poppy called.

"Quick Fran, where do you live?" implored St. John. She took a deep breath: "We live at..................." The door burst open.

Two men introduced themselves as police officers from Special Branch. They would be escorting the three to hospital. After that, a house arrest/witness protection plan would be put into effect. Further questioning would take place over the next few days by representatives from the Ministry of Defence. It transpired that two objects had been detected on radar. One had been a large object flying across their plane from west to east. The other had been a smaller object that, from its trajectory, had descended straight down from space and subsequently merged with the aircraft. The compromising of British air space by unidentified flying objects was a matter of national security.

Poppy and St. John had already glided out the door past the Special Branch officers and down the corridor to the exit. They both knew it was pointless hanging around any longer. They would get nowhere near Fran and Tony now. The moment had gone forever. Both were now suffering from the yearning for a love that had been lost before it had ever been gained. Thankfully, the positive thing was that they had convinced the trio not to tell on them. More importantly, at no time had they needed to mention the existence of the Golden Bluebell to the others. Fran and Tony, in particular, would be subjected to some very skilful interrogation, which might have got it out of them. The thought of any government getting hold of that magical flower and the power it held was as horrific as the thought of Stheno possessing it!

CHAPTER 4
RETURN TO HONEYPOT HILL

Outside, torrential rain was thundering down like a waterfall. The rain's force was multiplied by the raging west wind that had delivered it to south Leicestershire at Poppy's request. Poppy clapped her hands and exclaimed to the heavens. "Thank you Xanthus! Thank you Zephyr!"

"Are you off your rocker?" shouted St. John over the howl of the wind. "That's all we need right now." He was feeling agitated. The loss of Fran was getting to him already. "Anyway, what have they got to do with it?" he snapped.

"Andromeda got Mercury to deliver a message for me. I asked Xanthus to get his father, Zephyr, god of the West Wind, to do this as a favour," Poppy proudly replied. "And you're wrong. It's precisely what we do need! You'll see why later."

They rose into the sky, leaving the lights of East Midlands Airport and Fran and Tony behind them. Reluctantly, St. John directed the Golden Arrow south-east towards Honeypot Hill and ultimate Armageddon.

As St. John and Poppy touched down at the foot of Honeypot Hill, the west wind instantly dropped and the downpour abruptly ceased. Poppy surveyed the scene with satisfaction. A slight ridge, approximately three hundred metres out from the base of the hill, inconspicuously marked the line of a substantial dip. Years of accumulated silt within the dip had now been turned into a quagmire of mud which was hidden beneath a shallow depth of standing rainwater. Beyond that, the ever-widening triangle of the massive meadowland glistened with rainwater all the way to its base where Medusa's evil wild flowers grew. The undergrowth and trees lining the sides made the triangular field a perfect shape for funnelling any attackers charging the hill into a 'bunched' formation, thus making them easier targets. It was, for all intents and purposes, a replica of the site where the Battle of Agincourt took place in France on 25th October 1415 A.D.

"It is the right choice," murmured Poppy, thinking aloud. "I shall use the battle tactics of King Henry V."

"Who?" queried St. John, not quite hearing.

"King Henry the Fifth," confirmed Poppy. "Remember the historical account mum told us about the heavily outnumbered Good King Hal and his victory at Agincourt?"

"Who could forget?" replied St. John. "Mum always reckoned that one of our ancestors was a member of his famous band of archers. Always made me feel proud, that did. And I always respected the Yew tree more than ever after that."

"Exactly," replied his sister, "and, if the battle strategy was good enough for Henry, a great English warrior king, then it is good enough for Poppy, a child of the stars."

She smiled at the comparison and her tightly set lips betrayed an iron determination to live up to King Henry's reputation.

There was a rustling behind them, followed by the Pig bursting out of the bushes and pounding down towards his friends with tongue hanging out and eyes laughing with pleasure. Gliding behind him were Angelica, Bryony and Sorrel – the three White Archangels. Pig was jumping up and down, licking their feet and generally going berserk with happiness. St. John unhitched the lunch bag from the Golden Arrow and gave the conning dog the last piece of fruit pie from the Lares. A glint signalled a movement from the yellow dart. The Golden Arrow had slowly lifted and stood on its tail with the tip pointing towards the constellation of Orion. There was a slight quivering of its shaft, then whoosh! In the blink of an eye, it was just a gold speck of sand on the silver beach of the universe. As the speck faded, so did the electric-blue protective shield of Athena that surrounded the twins. Neither Poppy nor St. John required those aids from the gods any longer now that they were back on Earth.

The three White Archangels surrounded them. A flurry of tinkling bell sounds lilted back and forth from the angels as they asked Poppy about every detail of their adventure. When Poppy responded to their questions, the pitch of the bells rose higher and higher, firstly in fear and then in excitement at her replies.

"What are they saying?" interrupted St. John. He found it frustrating that he could not understand the wild flower language of the angels' in the way Poppy could.

"I'm just explaining about the purpose of Medusa's flowers," said Poppy. "It's come as a bit of a shock for them to find out what it is. I've also had to tell them everything about our journey. They had been extremely worried that something might have happened to us."

"Something might have happened to us?" gasped St. John. "That's got to be the great British understatement of the year!"

Poppy ignored his sarcastic protest. Her mind was miles away, deep in thought. She was making final adjustments to her overall battle strategy.

"Right," she said, "I'm calling a council of war. Everyone sit down in a circle. We haven't got too long before dawn and we've got a lot to do."

Poppy's voice had now become authoritative and commanding.

"I'll recapitulate on the situation and then I'll tell you what I need. First, the situation. Thanks to Electra's powers of vision, we now know the identity of Medusa's evil wild flowers and their capabilities if she had activated them. Currently, because of mythological events and the slaying of Medusa by Perseus, we also know that they will now be activated by the command of her Gorgon sister, Stheno, instead. All that's happened is that one vicious rat-bag has been replaced by another. As for the flowers of evil, when the White Archangels first took me down to the bottom of the meadow to show me, I estimated there were about five thousand of them. Medusa had given each one a coded name to keep their true identity and purpose a secret."

Poppy continued her summary. "According to Electra, the identity of the flowers and their role, after transformation, is as follows:

1. Giant Hogweed: These wild flowers will become three-metre high giant boars with bone-crunching jaws and flesh-tearing tusks.

2. Devilsbit Scabious: When the time comes, Stheno will call out their name and they will be transformed into screaming, scab-covered demons.

3. Crowfoot: These will become razor-beaked, flesh-tearing, eye-pecking crows, with claws like meat hooks.

4. Skullcap: Those flowers will become fighting skeletons armed with helmets, swords and shields. St. John and I already know how dangerous they can be from our experiences in the Arena of Death!

5. Deadly Nightshade: Finally, according to Electra, at Stheno's signal those wild flowers will become long-fanged, blood-sucking creatures of the night."

Poppy turned to St. John. "I have already told Angelica, Bryony and Sorrel that the objective of these monsters will be to seize the Golden Bluebell for Stheno so that she can force it to create a permanent winter all over the Earth. The result will be an everlasting Ice Age and all the beautiful wild flowers will die. Furthermore, every other living creature will perish along with them. I have already decided which of Mother Nature's wild flowers I will put up against them in our attempt to repulse the tyrant's attack. The angels will be taking me to the places where the flowers I have selected grow and I will muster the best army of volunteers that I can. Before I go with them, I need you to do something for me St. John while I'm gone. After that, your sole task is to kill Stheno."

St. John's hand subconsciously fondled the handle of Athena's sword that Perseus had loaned him. He was desperately holding on to his courage. The sword's presence bolstered his resolve. "I know what I have to do Poppy but I don't mind admitting that I'm scared at the thought already. Look, while you're out recruiting, do me a favour. I need to know Stheno's movements so that I can select a decent position near enough to her to strike. Will you rustle up twenty four sharp-eyed scouts to patrol the battlefield? Before you ask them to volunteer, I want you to ensure they realise it will be a suicide mission. Their success will surely mean their death. Meanwhile, tell me what you want doing and I'll get on with it. It will take my mind off the Gorgon."

Poppy pointed down the hill. "Okay. At the foot of the hill here, where the triangular meadow funnels into a bottleneck, is the start of a three hundred metre gentle slope of grass. Just beyond that is the wide dip, which as you know has been filled with the rain brought for me by Zephyr. I want you to build a line of fortification with long wooden stakes across the bottleneck. The line should be staggered in a series of 'V' shapes that jut out down the hill. The defences should be positioned directly in front of the water-filled dip on our hill side of it. I want the stakes to run continuously from the undergrowth and tree line that flanks the left-hand side of the field and across to the undergrowth and tree line that flanks the right. The stakes are to be rammed in the ground at forty five-degree angles and have sharpened tips. Leave intermittent gaps between them for sections of my army to advance through when the time comes. Oh yes, while you're at it, leave a fairly wide gap straight through the middle for my own use."

"Is that all!" responded St. John in amazement. "My name's Hayward, not Hercules you know. How, in God's name do you expect me to do all that by myself? Give me a box of matches to file my nails with," he jeered, "and I'll light a camp fire with them in my spare time. Don't be bloody ridiculous Poppy. Even if I could do it, have you thought about the fact that if your army - whatever the hell that is – can advance through the gaps I'm supposed to leave then Stheno's beasties can charge through the same gaps?"

Poppy tutted with annoyance. "Don't worry about the gaps; my tactics will cover that! Just trust me will you? Now, come with me," she ordered.

Poppy led St. John up the wooded hill and stood him near to the Yew tree. She then went off to move amongst the trees. Pressing her face to the bark of their trunks, Poppy was apparently talking to them.

"Flipping heck," thought St. John to himself, "she's definitely lost it this time. Me, three angels and a loopy dog led by a crazy woman against five thousand beasts from the bowels of hell led by an invincible monster. And what military might is she going to turn to for help in our darkest hour of need? ……………….A bunch of wild flowers!"

Poppy returned to him with purposeful strides. "Right, I have spoken to the Dryads – the forest nymphs that dwell within the trees. They are willing to donate four branches from each tree for your stakes. There is no need to cut them off; the trees will shed them for you. No problem there then!" she rebuked. St. John just stood there, dumbfounded. "Stay here by the Yew tree and keep out of the way!" instructed Poppy. "I'll be back in a bit." With that, she skipped off, leaving St. John speechless.

While he waited, St. John practised ramming Athena's polished bronze shield into the soft earth in one sweeping movement, so that its angled tilt gave a head-high reflection every time. Then he grasped Athena's sword with both hands and practised swinging it upwards and outwards in a wide arc across his body – from a vertical position at his right leg – to a horizontal head-high position on his left. He repeated this action until the sword always finished at head height by the time it had completed its one hundred and eighty degrees rising swing. After a while he sat down near the Yew tree and daydreamed about Fran. He had got it bad, that's for sure. Cupid had certainly 'punched his lights out'. His heart had more arrows in it than a pub dartboard. St. John had to smile to himself at his own self-ridiculing thoughts.

CHAPTER 5

THE SELECTION

Poppy reached the shallow flowing stream that ran along the foot of Honeypot Hill to the rear. There, she found the wild flowers she was looking for. Poppy had first spotted them on the day she visited the hill with St. John for a picnic. "That day seems so very long ago," she sighed to herself in tiredness as she moved along the water's edge. The wild flowers she now gently caressed were named Arrowhead, so called because of their arrow-shaped leaves. She knelt down and quietly whispered to them. Back came their tiny voices, which only Poppy could hear. She told her story, made her request and immediately received the unanimous vote of all two hundred volunteers.

Unfolding the letter that Flos had left for her with Electra, she read it again:

Dear Poppy Flos,
The names of the flowers will give you a clue.
To assemble your army, this you must do:
Sprinkle my potion and count loud – one, two, three.
Pick what you need and that is what they will be.
Your ever-watching,
Flos

Poppy took the dumpy glass bottle, labelled 'Essence of Enchanter's Nightshade' and sprinkled a few drops on the Arrowhead wild flowers.

She then counted out loud "one, two, three," and declared "you shall be my archers!"

After a short pause, the stems and leaves started to vibrate and the flowers of the Arrowhead plants began to shake violently. Poppy had seen enough; Flos' magic potion was working. She turned and scurried back up the hill to the waiting St. John.

He was still drifting in his dream world. It was a world where his soul was free to dive, with abandon, into the dark pools that were Fran's eyes.

"Dreaming about Fran are we?" laughed Poppy as she brushed by him.

"I suggest you shift your backside before you get flattened in the crush, lover-boy." Her words yanked St. John back to stark reality and for a moment he did not know where he was. It was similar to that dazed feeling you sometimes got as a kid when your whole being had been engrossed in a Saturday afternoon film matinee while safely ensconced in the darkness of a cinema theatre. Suddenly, it would be over and as you stepped outside onto the pavement into the glaring sunshine your distant mind would be dragged away from the fantasy world of the film and thrust back into the real world that it did not want to inhabit.

St. John stumbled out of the way as Poppy knelt in front of the Yew tree. She sprinkled one drop of Enchanter's Nightshade on its roots, counted out loud "one, two, three," and declared "you shall be my trusty longbows". Instantly, a fissure appeared in the tree bark and the hand of the resident Dryad shot out holding a longbow of strong, resilient Yew wood. There came a sound of tramping feet trudging up the hill. St. John turned to see two hundred archers in brown leather doublets. A leather belt, running across the chest of each, held a quiver full of arrows on their backs. The belt around each archer's waist held a dagger, mallet and metal spikes. As they marched past the Yew tree, the Dryad handed each one a longbow. When all had been armed, the archers lined up in five ranks in front of St. John to await his orders.

The whole thing caught him by surprise. All eyes were now looking at him. For a moment he was overcome with uncertainty but he realised his actions now would set the standard of discipline and strength of morale that Poppy would require from her army if she was to defeat the enemy. His memory searched recent history for a leadership figure that he could emulate. St. John selected images from wartime documentaries of General Sir Bernard Montgomery, leader of the British 8th Army during the Second World War. He picked up a long twig and tucked it under his arm to simulate a swagger-stick. Stepping up onto a rock outcrop, he motioned the archers to gather around him. In a loud, authoritative voice he addressed them:

"Make no mistake about our objective. I promise you nothing but blood, sweat and tears. Let there be no bellyaching. I will tolerate no bellyaching here! Nor will there be any hint of defeatism. The wild flowers of evil are not invincible – they can be vanquished. It can be done – and it will be done!"

Sweeping his swagger-stick from under his arm, he used it as an indicator to detail the plans of Poppy's fortifications. "Now I want stakes here, here, there, and over there." Poppy had to turn away to stop herself from laughing, although she knew that what St. John was doing was inspiring confidence in his men, both in themselves and in him.

After St. John had finished his briefing, as if on cue, a groaning and creaking could be heard throughout the woods. Tree branches, donated by the Dryad wood nymphs, started crashing down around them. The archers set to work dragging the branches to the intended positions, stripping them off with their daggers, sharpening one end, hammering them into the ground with their mallets and then sharpening the exposed tips.

"I'll see you later Napoleon," chuckled Poppy. "I'm off to join the angels."

"You'll join the real ones in Heaven if I get near you – you piddle-taking devil!" shouted St. John. She gave him a mock curtsy and disappeared.

Poppy rejoined Angelica, Bryony and Sorrel. "I have already decided on the wild flowers that will best make up our army," she informed them. "If I give you their names, will you please take me to where they grow and introduce me? Tell them I am looking for volunteers and what I will be asking them to do is dangerous, even fatal, but it is in the cause of Mother Nature and every other wild flower. I will explain the details and their role after you have conferred. Only then will I do the necessary metamorphosis if they agree." The first two wild flowers Poppy asked to speak to were the Coltsfoot and the Hardhead. Bryony and Sorrel went off to seek out the Hardheads.

Angelica took Poppy to an area of bare, clay ground where the Coltsfoot favoured growing. While Angelica made the introductions, Poppy studied the flowers. It was easy to see why, in olden days, people called them Coltsfoot because their leaves were shaped like the footprint of a horse's hoof. Angelica finished her briefing and all two hundred flowers volunteered down to the last one. Poppy drew near to explain her objective and the role she had for them. Having received their permission, she sprinkled them with the essence of Enchanter's Nightshade, counted out loud "one, two, three," and declared "you shall be the horses for my knights!"

The stems on the Coltsfoot began to quiver and their petals shook violently. Each flower started to contort and stretch out into a head and body. Their stems split into four to form the rough outline of legs. The shapes became a coloured blur of twisting pale yellow, mixed with green and red. Then the shapes just grew and grew amid the vibrant haze of colour. There was a flash of light and the distorted silhouettes consolidated into huge, powerful, shire horses. The mane and tail of each horse was plaited with twists of ribbon in the deep green and bright red colours of Mother Nature's crown of Holly. The saddle blankets on their backs and draped along the flanks was of a yellow hue that was the Coltsfoot's petal colour. The shire horses then jostled into lines and knelt down on their forelegs as Poppy passed

47

along the ranks to lovingly stroke their heads. It was their way of pledging allegiance to serve her. She curtsied before them in gracious acknowledgement.

Having talked to the Hardhead wild flowers, Bryony and Sorrel glided back to Poppy. She went with the angels and her shire horses dutifully followed behind. There, she knelt down and spoke to them. The faint hum of voices whispered their consent in Poppy's ears. She sprinkled her potion and declared "you, with your hardheads, will become my steel helmeted knights". The same trembling transformation took place and in a flash, two hundred knights stood before her. Each knight was arrayed in a suit of armour overlain with a surcoat in green and red. The 'hardheads' of their metal helmets sprouted plumes of the same purple colour as their flower petals.

Bryony stepped forward and gestured towards Poppy. "This is your leader. Do you pay homage and swear allegiance in the tradition of true knights?"

The knights went down on one knee and in unanimous voices declared: "We so swear our allegiance unto death!" Poppy's emotions were overwhelmed at the devotion shown by the wild flowers and felt the need to return the dedication. She pulled Athena's dagger from its sheath and slowly swept it in a wide arc over the bowed heads of her followers. The knights mounted their shire horses and Sorrel led them down to the fortifications.

At Poppy's request, Bryony went off to speak to the Tway Blade wild flowers, while Angelica took her to the Spear Thistles. They were very tall plants. Each leaf was edged with needle-sharp spines, like spears – hence their name. Angelica made her introductions then Poppy sprinkled Flos' magic liquid and proclaimed "you shall be my spearmen!" Again, came the violent shaking of the plants and the stems stretched to two metres tall. In an explosion of light, two hundred spearmen carrying long spears and rectangular shields appeared. Their bodies were draped in a protective covering of chain mail armour. Each shield bore the coat-of-arms of Mother Nature's crown. Angelica called them to attention and they all slung their spears, as one, onto their shoulders. The White Archangel then marched them off to the mustering area.

By now Sorrel had returned, having led the mounted knights down to the fortifications. Poppy took her hand lovingly and said: "Now, my dearest Sorrel, I have two other tasks for you. Will you find Pig and ask him to come to me. Tell him I will give him a whole packet of ginger biscuits. That will make him take notice! Then gather three more types of wild flowers for me. I shall want one plant that is named Bugle and twenty four Autumn Hawkbit flowers. For my third, I shall require twenty Ground Ivy plants – I think they should be sufficient. Tell them that they will be keeping their form as Ground Ivy and will not be fighting but I will enhance their main feature for an important part in my battle strategy. Sorrel flew off down the hill to carry out Poppy's requests.

As Sorrel left, Bryony flitted back from having located and spoken to as many Tway Blade wild flowers as she could find. "I have explained everything to them," reported Bryony, "and they are keen to speak to you and find out the role you wish them to perform".

"Good," replied Poppy. "We must hurry. Dawn will soon be here and the attack by Stheno will come any time after that. There are still things I must do to be ready." Bryony glided off to a damp part of the woods where the Tway Blades grew and towed Poppy behind her. The flowers were waiting and babbled excitedly among themselves as they speculated on what Poppy would turn them into.

These flowers are one of the British orchid families but the feature that most served Poppy's immediate needs were the two broad leaves that grew at the base of each stem. It is from those pairs of leaves that the Tway Blade gets its name, i.e. from the Old English word 'Twa', meaning 'Two'.

Poppy explained the form their transition would take and all two hundred eagerly gave their consent. She sprinkled drops of the Enchanter's Nightshade over them and declared "each of you will be a man-at-arms". The Tway Blades underwent the same metamorphosis and as the blinding flash of white light dimmed, Poppy saw two hundred men-at-arms standing before her.

At the time she applied the magic potion Poppy had selected in her mind the picture of the men-at-arms that had fought at Agincourt. She had chosen well. The men-at-arms standing before her were a frightening sight. They were clad from head to foot in impenetrable armour. On the right side of their belts hung an extra long-bladed dagger and on the left a broad sword. While the long dagger was wielded with the left hand, the sword was wielded with the right. However, the broad sword had an extra long handle so that when required, it could be gripped with two hands to give enormous force to sweeping blows from the weapon. These 'knights on foot' also carried other devastating weapons, such as the battle-axe and mace, for smashing their opponents to the ground. With both their daggers and swords (Tway Blades) smashing and slashing as they trundled forward, combined with their armour plating, the men-at-arms were truly the mediaeval 'tanks' of their time. Bryony lined the foot knights into three ranks and led them off to the rendezvous point.

By now, Angelica had returned to Poppy accompanied by the Pig. He nuzzled up to Poppy in expectation of the packet of ginger biscuits that she had falsely promised him then slumped to the ground in disappointment. However, he soon perked up and wagged his tail when Poppy told him that she was going to make him a leader and 'Top Dog'. He bounded along beside Angelica as she floated Poppy to the grassy, wooded place where her final selection of wild flowers liked to grow. She explained her intentions and plan to them. They all agreed to her requests – particularly the last one which asked them to acknowledge Pig as their leader. Pig sat wagging his tail and sticking out his chest with pride when he heard this. However, his task was to have a mixed sweet and sour flavour about it. On the sour side, little did he realise that he was in for a big problem! On the sweeter side, he was about to discover that there was something in life that was a thousand times more sugary than a packet of ginger biscuits.

Poppy leaned over and sprinkled her potion over the cluster of two hundred purple wild flowers, known as Dog Violets. The magic formula's cycle of transformation took place. Following the flash of white light a long silence ensued as the newly-metamorphosed objects looked at Poppy, then at Pig and then at each other.

"I'm off while the going's good," Poppy told Pig. "You know what I require from you and your new team. So, I'll leave it with you 'leader'." She laughed and flew off with Angelica and Sorrel who had returned after gathering the three different wild flowers that Poppy had asked for.

The two angels glided Poppy to the foot of a Chestnut tree where Sorrel had laid out the twenty four Autumn Hawkbits, twenty Ground Ivy plants and one Bugle flower. St. John waited with the gathered flowers for Poppy's arrival. She knelt over the twenty four Autumn Hawkbit flowers with her potion.

"Before you perform your magic," said St. John, "will you tell them something for me please Poppy? Tell them that I admire their courage in volunteering for a mission, which only rewards them with certain death if they are successful. I want them to know that I am proud to regard them as my blood brothers." In a solemn gesture, he drew Athena's sword, nicked his thumb and dripped his blood over their petals. From that day forward it can be seen that Autumn Hawkbit wild flowers carry, with pride, a red tinge on the underside of their outer petals as a badge of honour.

Poppy sprinkled Flos' liquid, and stated: "You shall be St. John's spotter hawks." Following the flurry of transformation, twenty-four hawks were fluttering around his feet and sitting on his shoulders. Next, Poppy weaved her magic and transformed the Bugle flower into her own personal herald to trumpet out her signals of command. The herald appeared, dressed in white breeches and gold jacket. He stood proudly to attention in front of Poppy with his golden bugle held high. Next, Poppy sprinkled the powerful juice on the Ground Ivy plants and decreed: "You shall retain your present form but your natural powers of creeping growth will increase a thousand fold!" The flowers quivered as the power of rapid growth was magically instilled within them.

Poppy asked Sorrel to take the Ground Ivy and plant them in the central gap of the fortifications left for her by St. John. Sorrel hurried away with the plants and St. John returned to the fortifications with the angel. His screeching hawks fluttered excitedly around him and the following herald was impatiently waving his arm about to stop the birds from landing on his precious golden bugle. After they had gone, Angelica turned to Poppy and observed: "That appears to be everything done that needs to be done. We are ready now to face the wrath of Stheno. Is there anything else I can do for you?"

"Is there a quiet clearing in the woods somewhere?" asked Poppy. "There is something I want to do and I need to be alone." Angelica guided her to a secluded place and left Poppy there in deep contemplation.

Chapter 6
The Pig

Meanwhile, Pig stood alone and looked at his new charges. As he tried to get to grips with the responsibilities bestowed upon him, all hell broke loose. Two hundred dogs of all breeds, shapes and sizes suddenly started bickering with each other. There was much snarling and gnashing of teeth. As Pig padded up and down deciding whether to rant at them or bite a few ears, a rather silky, well-educated voice whispered in his ear from behind:

"I think it would be a good idea if you firstly separated the bitches from the dogs. Half the disputes between the males are over possession of the females; they're nearly as bad as the humans are. Secondly, you need to separate them into groups of their own breed; they might get on a lot better with their own kind. Any disagreements after that will have to be settled by you. I'm sure you can manage it – after all, you look like a big strong lad."

The last comment that the voice made had a certain salacious overtone to it.

Pig turned around to look straight into a pair of big, brown, inviting eyes. His eyeballs bulged and his tongue flopped out. The vision was more inviting than a wide open grocery cupboard. Standing before him was a female golden Labrador who, as a former 'Dog Violet', was aptly named Violetta. He did not know whether to stand on his tail or his head. What he finally did do was to gather himself together by pulling his stomach in, puffing his chest out and clearing his voice to say "much obliged ma'am" in his deepest growl. He also quickly wiped a front paw across his mouth to hide the tell-tale drools of saliva that threatened to give away his raging desire. If Tony and St. John thought they had 'got it bad' over Poppy and Fran, they'd seen nothing yet when it came to Pig's maelstrom of feelings.

Taking Violetta's advice, he barged into the melee and firmly separated the ladies from the not-so-gentle gentlemen. After that, it was easier to get in among the dogs and 'throw a few wobbles' at them until he got a bit of silence. Pig threatened to hand out a battering following a small amount of grief from a couple of British Bulldogs. Fortunately for Pig, they backed down after he initially stood his ground and followed it up by reminding them that their illustrious leader, Poppy, had appointed him as leader. Pig heaved a sigh of relief when they bowed to Poppy's authority. "Thank the Lord for that," he thought to himself. "They're stubborn cusses but I'd rather have one of them protecting my back than any other dog."

Pig was right to think like that. The Bulldog was one of the oldest of British breeds. Down through the ages and up to the eighteenth century it was mainly used for bull baiting – hence its name. The overhang of its lower jaw, beyond the line of teeth in its upper jaw, enabled it to cling to the bull's muzzle with an interlocking bite that was impossible to break apart even (it was reputed) when it was dead! It was a surly and unsociable animal but possessed indomitable courage.

Having finally attained a semblance of order and settled the leadership question, Pig got the dogs into their breed formations. They were a right motley collection of teeth, muscle and pure guts. There were Alaskan Eskimo dogs, Bull Terriers, Great Danes, Otter Hounds, Mastiffs, Newfoundland dogs, Scottish Deerhounds, Saint Bernards, Irish Wolfhounds, Chows, Dalmatians, Pointers, Foxhounds, Greyhounds, Bloodhounds, English Sheepdogs, Russian Borzois and, of course, the proverbial 'Who ya looking at sonny?' British Bulldogs. While he was doing that, he noticed that Violetta had taken the initiative and done the same for him with the bitches. Moreover, she had made a damned good job of it. He was just as full of admiration for her 'dogged' personality as he was for her female charms. Pig stood back to survey his pack. "Stone a crow," he thought to himself, "what a lean, mean, killing machine. Let's face it, who'd want to meet them up a dark alley?"

Once discipline had been achieved, Pig thought it would be a good opportunity to chat-up Violetta. The realisation was now dawning on him that he would actually consider giving this girl his last ginger biscuit. For Pig, this act would be the ultimate definition of true love. He was shocked to realise that he would actually do it! As Violetta sloped towards him in a very erotic snaking movement, his bulging eyeballs were dragged away to the pack of dogs again. A general howl had gone up amongst the ranks. There were complaints being raised of an uncomfortable and peculiar pressured feeling in the nether regions. Pig had not thought of this until now. They were formerly wild flowers, so they would not know about such things; they needed a pee! Out of a sense of decency, he asked Violetta to deal with the bitches, while he dealt with the challenge of the dogs. He lined them up in two rows and stood in front to explain the reason for their discomfort and then give a demonstration of what to do about it.

The exercise was a complete disaster. The front line cocked a back leg so that they were now balanced on three limbs. Unfortunately, the Great Dane on the extreme right lost his balance and fell over against the next one. The whole line tumbled over like a row of dominoes. The rear rank had cocked their legs with perfect balance. The only problem was that some had cocked their left leg, whilst others had cocked their right. Everyone got caught in a devastating crossfire. For one's personal safety, it is not good practice to even dare give a British Bulldog a sideways glance, let alone for a Great Dane to pee on its head from a great height. Consequently, all hell broke loose again and there were 'snarl-ups' all over the place.

Pig finally sorted it out and to keep their minds off bickering and backbiting all the time he set them the task of practising their combat tactics. He split the animals into fighting units of three. Two were to go for the legs of the enemy and bring them down, while the third was to dive in and go for the throat of the floored victim. He left them repeating the exercise whilst he drew Violetta to one side and suggested they go to a quite part of the woods to talk tactics. He found a suitable place and they sat down. He proposed that she should be his deputy because she had the brains. She also had the looks but he didn't mention that at this stage; best not to rush things and ruin his chances. He told Violetta that Poppy had wanted the pack to be split into two fighting units on opposite sides of the battlefield and he felt that she had the acumen to lead the bitches. Violetta agreed to take on the responsibility. All the while Pig was talking she had been watching him closely. He was a powerfully-built specimen of a dog with a commanding personality. Yet belying that was a hidden sensitivity that his eyes were now betraying in her presence. His eyes briefly caught Violetta's gaze and he turned away in uncomfortable embarrassment. This softer side of his character was totally new to him and he was finding it highly confusing.

Then Violetta asked a question that sent him in a panic: "Why do you have such a disparaging name as Pig?" He was out to impress this high-class lady. How could he explain the meaning of 'Pig by name – Pig by nature' and how he was renowned for eating anything that didn't move and biting anything that did? Or how he had a reputation for being pig-headed because he took no notice of anyone and did what the hell he liked? The only positive thing he could say to counter all those negatives was that people looked upon him as a 'loveable rogue', which was not the most endearing attribute to knock her flat!

Pig wracked his brains for a plausible explanation and found it – thanks to St. John. He remembered sitting at the young man's feet by the fireside one night at Aunt Kay's, listening to him spouting on about mythology stories and thinking what a boring old fart he was. Pig had sat wagging his tail and feigning an interest in what St. John was saying because he was hoping he could con a biscuit from him for such attentive behaviour. Luckily, one story had stuck in the dog's mind – the legend of Galatea. Now it was going save the Pig's bacon!

He related to Violetta how, in the distant days of Roman mythology when the gods still took an interest in mankind, there lived a sculptor named Pygmalion. He had carved the statue of a woman from a block of stone. She looked so real and so beautiful to him that he actually fell in love with her and named her Galatea. The trouble was he could not cuddle a block of stone, no matter how lovely it looked. Each time he went into his studio, the gorgeous Galatea stood there looking at him and it was driving him crazy. It reached the stage where he ate with her, read to her and talked to her all day. At night he could not bear to go home and be parted from his Galatea, so he started sleeping on the floor of the studio, just to be beside her.

One night, in desperate longing, he threw himself on his knees and prayed to the Roman goddess, Venus, to put him out of his misery. Venus could easily have punished him for daring to create such a thing of beauty, which only the gods had the right to do. However, Venus happened to be the Roman goddess of love and she took pity on him. So, she bestowed on the statue of Galatea the gift of life and both she and Pygmalion lived happily ever after.

The cunning dog then bent the truth and said that his full name was really Pygmalion, but it was cut short to Pyg and the silly humans had spelt it wrongly as Pig. His final words to her were a flattering stroke of genius. "When I saw you standing there like a beautiful statue, my darling Violetta, I immediately knew that you were my Galatea. I would have spent eternity praying night and day to Venus to give you the gift of life so that I could hold you in my paws." Those poetic words soon had Violetta nuzzling up to him.

It was quite some time before the pair returned to the main group. There was much nudging and winking between the pack as Pig and Violetta led them down to the fortifications.

CHAPTER 7
AURIGA'S FAVOUR

After Angelica had withdrawn, Poppy stood alone in the forest clearing gazing up at the moonlit, star-sprinkled, night sky. She knew that Mercury had delivered her plea to Zephyr because the lashing rain had been delivered by the great wind, right on time. Now she desperately hoped that Mercury had delivered her messages to Athena and Auriga, the heavenly charioteer. She took a deep breath, held high Andromeda's Ring of Friendship and cried out to the stars:

"Invincible Auriga, please grant the favour that I have asked of you. Mighty Athena, I beg you to use your great powers to deliver Auriga's favour to me!"

The crystal clear diamonds of Andromeda's ring suddenly burst into a radiant electric blue. From an empty black patch in the sky appeared a faint, tiny ball of blue light. As Poppy watched, the blue fireball grew larger and larger as it hurtled down from the heavens towards her. The low rumbling sound that accompanied it rose into a roaring crescendo. The crackling blue sphere of lightning was so blinding that Poppy had to put her hands over her eyes. Even then, she could still see the stark blue light through her screwed-up eyelids. The searing radiance that was Athena's pure power hovered for a few seconds. Then, as quickly as it had appeared, it instantly ceased. Poppy now stood in the middle of the clearing in darkness and total silence. She hardly dare open her eyes.

Then a smile came to her lips and her arms relaxed to her sides at the sound of the gentle words that were next whispered to her. "Hello Poppy, my dearest friend and child of the stars. I knew you could not bear to be parted from us."

Poppy laughed. She would know that voice anywhere – it was Xanthus! She opened her eyes, ran to him and threw her arms around his neck. Xanthus nuzzled up to one cheek as Balius snuggled up against her other.

"My lovely, beautiful horses," murmured Poppy as she kissed their noses. "Been in any good fights to the death recently?" asked Xanthus. Then he neighed with laughter.

"No, but there's a humdinger coming at a theatre-of-war near you and I've been lumbered for the part of leading-lady," Poppy jibed back at him.

"Yes, Balius and I know all about it," replied Xanthus in a more serious tone. "Auriga has told us. Oh, by the way, as well as sending us along to help, he also sends his regards. He said to tell you that his offer still stands; you are welcome in the heavens and to his constellation anytime you like so that you can drive around the skies and exercise his teams of horses. They miss you."

"Yes and I miss them as well," replied Poppy in remembered affection.

"Auriga is a bit of a 'strong silent type' you know," observed Xanthus, "but I know that he misses you too. When Athena came to collect Balius and myself, Auriga was already halfway through building you this – your own chariot of silver. He meant it when he said he would be proud to adopt both of you as his son and daughter. Now then, before you get too embarrassed, take a look at a couple of extras he has supplied."

Poppy inspected the shining chariot. It was carrying an extra supply of fearsome weaponry but even more frightening were the additions to the wheels. Razor-sharp scythe blades, one metre in length, had been bolted to the hubs of the wheels and would mutilate anything that stood in their path.

"Perhaps you hadn't noticed, or you're too nice to say, but have you taken a good look at us?" asked Xanthus. "We feel like a couple of out-of-work unicorns, don't we Balius?" Balius curled his lip in agreement.

Poppy took a good look at the horses and it was obvious what Xanthus meant. Auriga had fitted a metal plate to their foreheads, from which extended a long steel spike.

"So, what would madam like?" Xanthus enquired in a haughty voice. "Would madam like us to skewer a few monsters through the guts, or would she care for us to toast her some tea-cakes?"

"I think we'll stick to the monsters for now," replied Poppy in a tone of mock nonchalance. "I'm afraid that under the pressing circumstances of the forthcoming engagement, I have a limited appetite."

With that, Poppy jumped onto the chariot. "Come my beauties, let us now go and join my army." With that, she lightly shook the reins and the faithful horses trotted off towards the battlefield.

On the way, Xanthus gave Poppy a message from Electra, which shook her composure to the core. Electra's gift of inner-sight had given her a vision of foreboding but the picture was unclear and blocked by a screen of evil spun by Hecate. All Electra could do was to give a warning that someone dear to Poppy's heart would betray her and thus cause her death. She was stunned. The faces of all those close to her ran through Poppy's mind. She dismissed each one in turn as being totally above suspicion.

"I have no idea who it could possibly be my dear Xanthus," she said with a frown. "But there is nothing I can do about it now. The game's afoot and I have to play it through to the end." With that, she snapped the reins and the horses carried Poppy to her destiny.

CHAPTER 8
THE ORDER OF BATTLE

The bright moonlight glinted upon the silver chariot as Xanthus and Balius galloped around the base of Honeypot Hill and into the assembly area behind the fortification of wooden stakes. Poppy reined-up beside St. John and came to a halt in front of her army of one thousand strong. Together, the twin brother and sister made a resplendent sight. Poppy stood proud on Auriga's chariot. She confidently held the reins to her two powerful snorting horses, which pawed at the ground and champed at their bits. The moonbeams shimmered upon her white diaphanous Grecian gown with its silk embroidered pattern of interlaced red poppies. The moon's glow caused the jewelled handle of Athena's dagger, in its gold sheath, to sparkle. Poppy's long raven hair, set against the white of her gown, contrasted like night and day. The contrast was enhanced by the ribbon of Arachne's pure white thread, studded with glittering emeralds, with which Electra had tied her tresses. The ribbon bore the symbolic colours of Electra that she requested Poppy carry into battle as a token of her favour. Poppy now wore the ribbon with as much pride as she did the crown of flowers upon her head. The many coloured petals of her wild flower diadem, freshly shining from the morning dew, had been made by Flos herself and Poppy drew strength from the honour bestowed upon her by her ancestral family.

St. John stood beside Xanthus. His feet were set firmly apart, head held high and hand resting on the hilt of Athena's sword.

The polished bronze shield of the goddess reflected the yellow St. John's Wort wild flower embroidered on his Grecian tunic and the emerald-studded ribbon that Electra had tied to his arm in token of her favour. At the sight of their leaders the army cheered.

Poppy's mind raced through the deployment positions for the final time.

Her chariot would be positioned centrally and directly behind the wooden stakes. The archers, led by Bryony, were to be lined across the assembly area behind Poppy.

Hidden in the tree line at the foot of the hill, would be the two hundred spearmen, led by Angelica. Concealed further back behind the spearmen was to be the two hundred men-at-arms, which Poppy intended to lead when she judged the moment to be right.

Sorrel, appointed to lead the two hundred knights, was to split them into two groups and hide them behind the tree line, halfway down the meadow, on the left and right flanks.

The dog pack, similar to the knights, was also to be split into two groups, left and right, but positioned level with the mud-filled ditch.

The hawks were under the total control of St. John. Poppy was acutely aware that no matter how courageous she and her army might be in combat that day, if her brother failed to slaughter Stheno, they would lose the battle – and the good planet Earth.

Poppy now turned and addressed her army. "I have allocated each regiment's leader a personal signal. Under no circumstances will they leave position or attack the enemy until I give the command. When I do this, their personal signal to join the battle will be trumpeted by my herald. I must point out that from my estimates, we are outnumbered by five to one but we can still win this battle. We *must* win this battle! However, because of the odds against us, the only way we can do this is through tactical surprise, timing and discipline."

Poppy's Battle Plan

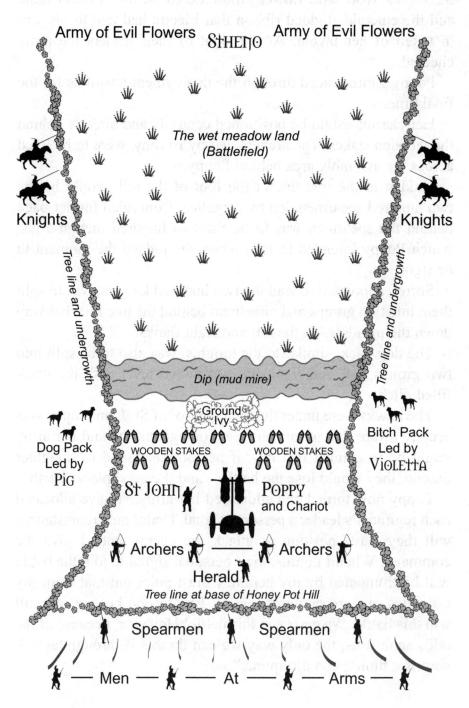

Army of Evil Flowers Stheno Army of Evil Flowers

*The wet meadow land
(Battlefield)*

Knights   Knights

Tree line and undergrowth   Tree line and undergrowth

Dip (mud mire)

Ground
Ivy

Dog Pack
Led by
Pig

WOODEN STAKES   WOODEN STAKES

Bitch Pack
Led by
Violetta

St John   Poppy
and Chariot

Archers   Archers

Herald

Tree line at base of Honey Pot Hill

Spearmen   Spearmen

— Men — At — Arms —

"Aye," shouted a man-at-arms as he raised his sword, "and a length of cold steel with some flower power behind it!" A roar of approval for his words went up from the ranks.

Poppy smiled at his gesture of defiance and waited for the troops to settle.

"And now," she said calmly, "before this day begins, let each of us take time in silent prayer for courage to face the trials to come. Give thought to the burden of responsibility we carry for the preservation of all wild flowers of the world and our duty to our queen, Mother Nature, as custodians of her many gifts."

CHAPTER 9
STHENO'S ARMY

As Poppy and St. John's army stood in silence, Aurora, Roman goddess of the dawn, sent the first rays of daybreak slanting across Honeypot Hill. With it, from the distant end of the meadow, came the scream from hell that marked the arrival of Stheno.

Oblivious to anything except her evil intent, Stheno moved among the five thousand wild flowers sown by her dead sister with vile relish. First, in the name of Medusa, she commanded the Giant Hogweed to rise up. This plant, with its pink and white flowers, grows exceptionally tall and can be poisonous to the touch. Medusa had given it this property so as to provide protection while it grew to its full height. A grey cloud slowly drifted upwards from their roots and in the haze rose the putrid stench of corruption. As the cloud cleared, milling around within its midst, were one thousand huge hogs. Their black hairy bodies stood three metres high with grating jaws, bone-crunching teeth and flesh-tearing tusks. The frenzied bellows of the giant boars ripped through the stillness of the dawn to carry up the meadow to Honeypot Hill. A shiver of fear ran up the spines of Poppy's army as they stood in silent prayer.

Stheno cackled with satisfaction at the wickedness of Medusa and marvelled at her sister's twisted innovation. Next, she moved amongst the bright blue flowers of the Devilsbit Scabious, which looked so deceivingly pretty and innocent. In the name of Medusa, her Gorgon sister commanded them to rise up. Again, a

66

cloud arose and as the grey mist vanished, a thousand screaming, horned devils leapt up from the ground. Their slimy blue bodies were blotched with scabs and poison-weeping sores. The demons whirled around in a dance of death. As they lashed their long tails from side to side, the hooked barbs at their tips made a swishing sound, like a guillotine slicing down towards the neck of its victim. Simultaneously, the screams of the devils echoed across the meadow and sliced through the hearts of Poppy's army.

Stheno chuckled in amusement at their antics as she moved on towards the carpet of Crowfoot flowers. She performed the same ritual of command and a thousand enormous crows fluttered up from a stinking cloud as it rolled away across the field. Their scissors-like beaks and bear-trap claws were capable of tearing off heads and shredding limbs.

Next, she moved among the Skullcaps and at her exhortations a thousand fighting skeletons sprang from the earth. The helmeted, bony figures rattled themselves into formation and stood poised with shields held high and short swords thrust forward. At Stheno's orders there was a teeth-rattling clatter as the skeletons slammed their heel bones together and came to attention.

Finally, Stheno slid her way through the mass of Deadly Nightshade and from the murk of swirling gas, three-metre high figures could be seen arising. The cloud dissipated to reveal a thousand blood-sucking, deadly creatures of the night. They had long arms for gripping their victims whilst sinking fangs into the necks of their prey to drain the entire body of blood. The creatures' limbs were muscular but their pink translucent bodies were thin. However, folds of jelly-like flesh hung from their torsos. This was to allow their bodies to bloat up as they sucked their fill from the poor writhing souls whose lives were slowly ebbing away. The monsters were a repulsive sight. After they had feasted on the blood of several victims, their pink flesh would turn deep red. The odd purple lumps that would eventually be seen floating around their bellies in the forthcoming battle were clots of victim's blood, yet to be digested. When sated and bloated, their red, wobbling bodies became nightmare strawberry jellies from the moulds of Hades. Even the thousand serpents that grew from the head of Stheno reared back and hissed at them in revulsion.

In the distance, at the top end of the meadow, Poppy's army still stood at the foot of the hill in silent meditation. Yet, as the rising tide of screams, cackles and roars washed over them on the dawn's breeze, Poppy sensed the unease and fear that was beginning to spread amongst her troops. She leaned over the side of the chariot and whispered to St. John:

"They are beginning to lose heart. Say something to raise their spirits."

"Like what?" snapped St. John, "England's just won the World Cup!"

The tension was now getting to the pair of them.

"Don't be so bloody daft!" she spat back. "What about the pre-battle Agincourt speech that King Henry V gave his army? You know, the one from Shakespeare's play Henry the Fifth. You reckoned you'd learned it off by heart after mum told us she thought one of our ancestors had been one of King Henry's archers at the Battle of Agincourt. We have to try something. Now damn well do it!"

St. John protested that he was not sure whether he could adapt Shakespeare's version of the speech to fit the current situation. Their bickering was interrupted by Angelica's worried plea: "Oh, that we had here but one ten thousand of the wild flowers in Britain that sleep soundly in their beds with petals closed."

Her cry goaded St. John to leap up onto the chariot beside Poppy. He brandished Athena's sword and told Poppy to slowly parade her chariot up and down in front of her army.

"Smile at them girl," he told her. "Give out bags of confidence. Don't let them see that we're peeing our pants as well."

Poppy raised a clenched fist in a gesture of defiance and eased her horses forward.

Then St. John began to recite his own adapted version of Henry's speech.

"What's this you say dear Angelica? No, my fair Archangel, if we are marked to die, we are enough to do the countryside loss.

And if to live, the fewer the flowers – the greater the share of honour!

God's will, Angelica, I pray thee wish not one wild flower more.

Rather proclaim it, through my good will, that he that hath no stomach for this feast then let him depart. His absence shall be excused and money for his travel put into his purse.

We would not die in that man's company that fears his fellowship to die with us!

This day shall be called the 'Feast of Mother Nature'.

He that outlives this day and comes safe home will stand a-tip-toe when this day is named and rouse him at the name of Mother Nature.

He that shall live this day and see old age will yearly on the vigil, feast his neighbours and say: 'Tomorrow is Mother Nature's Day.'

Then, will he strip his sleeve and show his scars and say: 'These wounds I had on Mother Nature's Day.'

Old men forget, yet all shall be forgotten, but he will remember, with advantages, what feats he did this day.

Then shall our names, as familiar in his mouth as household words – Poppy, our leader, Angelica, Sorrel, Bryony and Pig – be in their flowing cups freshly remembered.

This story shall the good wild flowers tell their seedlings and Mother Nature's Day shall not go by from this day forth, to the ending of the world, but we in it shall be remembered.

We few. We happy few. We band of brothers!

For he today that sheds his blood with me shall be my brother, be he ne'er so base.

And wild flowers in Britain, now abed, shall think themselves accursed that they were not here and hold their conservation cheap in the presence of those that speak, who fought with us on Mother Nature's Daaaay!"

St. John's last bellowed word to the heavens, marking an end to his speech, brought forth a roar of defiance from the ranks that rose to meet the dawn.

Poppy seized the moment of her army's renewed resolve. "You know what you have to do. Now, to your positions! May the Great One bless you all." Then, under her breath, Poppy murmured to herself "and deliver us from evil".

Sorrel sent half her knights down the left flank of the field to weave their horses in and out of the trees to a hidden position halfway down the battlefield. She led the other half down the right flank and did the same. Pig gave Violetta a last nuzzle before he led his pack of dogs through the woods on the left and she led her bitches down to the right. Angelica led her spearmen out of sight into the tree line at the foot of the hill and at Poppy's order, the men-at-arms turned and followed. They passed through the lines of spearmen and assembled behind them. Poppy gave a gentle shake to the reins and Xanthus and Balius wheeled the chariot around to centre her just behind the defences. St. John took his place to her left. His hawks remained grounded around him - silently watching his every move. Bryony lined up her two hundred archers behind Poppy and took a position to their rear. She had not yet instructed them to string their bows and so they stood casually leaning upon their staffs of stout Yew wood. Some of the archers busied themselves honing their daggers, while others adjusted the flights to their arrows. The gold-coated herald stood to the rear of them and never took his eyes off Poppy. He was taut with anticipation at her command to trumpet the first signal.

Chapter 10

The Battle

Stheno gathered the seething mass of her five thousand beasts and divided each throng into their one thousand strong groups. Only now did she bother to take a good look at her objective. Honeypot Hill – with the ultimate power of Mother Nature's Golden Bluebell nestling on top – stood out plainly against the background of dawn. The glow of sunrise was now sufficient for her to see the adversary that Hecate had warned would stand between her and total power over the Earth. When she saw her enemy she screamed with laughter. "This has got to be a joke of the gods," she thought. "A stupid slip of a human girl – dressed up like Queen-of-the-May – atop a horse and cart; some naive misguided boy and a slovenly bunch of peasants lounging on bean-sticks." The more she looked, the more she laughed. Stheno did not need the whole of her evil host after all. She would send her giant boars to rampage up the field. In her assessment, amateurs had obviously erected the wooden stakes. There were gaps big enough to drive an elephant through, let alone her giant boars. They would clear those easily then trample over the motley collection of deluded idiots that stood in the way. A quick gallop to smash through the woods up to the top of the hill and the Golden Bluebell was hers. Stheno screamed at the boars to charge.

Poppy saw the beasts commence their careering run in the distance. Without taking her eyes off the onslaught sweeping up

71

the meadow towards her, Poppy reached across her trembling body and drew Athena's dagger from its sheath. In one sweep she brought her right arm straight out in a horizontal position at her side and held it there. This was the very first of a long line of signals that she would be giving in the implementation of her battle plans. It was now her wits against Stheno's revenge. Poppy noticed, with surprise, that now the battle had started her nervous shake had gone and the hand that held the dagger no longer trembled. Her confidence increased when the drawing of her dagger brought a rustle of movements behind her. The archers now leaned upon their bows to compress the springy Yew wood. In one move, all two hundred archers strung their bows. As they released the pressure from the long lengths of Yew, there came a low throbbing hum as the cords snapped taut.

The thousand giant boars roared on. The gobs of saliva that flew from their gaping jaws under the strain of their pounding gallop hung like strings of phlegm-coated pearls across their heaving chests. To stand before the thundering stampede of death and hold your ground was a terrifying ordeal. Poppy estimated that the beasts had now covered the first third of the meadow. At this point, she swept her arm high above her head and held it there. The long silver blade of Athena's dagger burst into a radiant glitter of electric blue. At this signal, the archers reached back to their quivers, pulled an arrow and slotted it to the cords. At a flick of the dagger, the archers raised their longbows and drew them back to their maximum tension. With every muscle and sinew straining, the archers maintained that position.

Poppy's upright arm remained perfectly still whilst her left hand joggled the reins of her horses. She cooed soothingly to Xanthus and Balius to keep patience as they champed at the bit to get at the enemy. The pounding boars were now two thirds of the way up the battlefield. Mixed feelings of fear and exhilaration swept through Poppy at the same time. "This," she thought, "is how King Henry V must have felt at the start of the Battle of Agincourt." She gritted her teeth and murmured to herself: "I must keep my nerve like he did." Despite Poppy's feverish thoughts, her self-discipline allowed her mind to continue calculating the closing distance between her and the rolling waves of heaving fur.

Bryony stood amid her archers and watched Poppy's glinting dagger intently. Suddenly, Poppy's arm cut sharply down to her side.

"Fire!" yelled Bryony at the top of her voice. There was a whoosh! It was as though an express train had just burst out of a tunnel. Then a hail of arrows shot high over the battlefield like a sheet of black slanting rain. The darts seemed to hang momentarily in mid-air and then plummet downward like a crashing ceiling of limestone stalactites. High-pitched squeals from the boars rose alongside geysers of erupting blood. The leading two hundred beasts were cut down as the steel tipped arrows split skulls, severed spines and smashed through ribs to embed themselves in lungs, livers and kidneys. Bryony hovered in front of her archers. "Reload!" she yelled. "Mark your targets!" The archers slotted new arrows, drew back their longbows and fine-tuned their calculated distance and trajectory. They held steady in abeyance to Bryony's final order. The White Archangel waited until the second wave of boars had clambered over the dead and writhing bodies of the fallen leaders. Again she yelled "Fire!" Another swarm of arrows flew over Poppy's head and fell as a descending theatre curtain upon the stage of death. A further two hundred boars were cut down in similar manner. "Yes", thought Poppy as she steadied her impatient horses, "it is exactly like the story of Agincourt that mum told us. The sky has indeed turned black with arrows."

As Poppy eyed the hail of arrows in awe, St. John was carefully watching the twelve hawks he had launched at the start of the charge of the boars. True to his orders, the hawks had been patrolling up and down the battlefield with eyes fixed directly down only on the ground over which they were instantly passing. Already, one hawk had turned to stone and dropped to the earth at the bottom of the meadow on the right flank. Then another had turned to stone and plunged to a spot, which was still at the bottom, but now more centrally placed at the meadow's base. St. John felt satisfaction and a sense of control over his situation now that he held intelligence on his opponent's movements. Simultaneously, he felt pangs of guilt at being personally responsible for instigating the deaths of those brave hawks and even braver wild flowers that they had once been.

"It's not fair, why me?" he muttered to himself as he wiped a tear from his eye.

"Because you're here lad and there's no one else," whispered a voice in his head. "You show me the big book where it states that life has to be fair."

St. John spun around but there was not a soul near him; everyone was staring up at the firework display of arrows streaking across the sky. No one saw the little god of the countryside, Pan, as he disappeared back into the bushes as quick as a flash.

As Poppy watched the second wave of arrows winging over, Bryony was already hovering in front of her archers to organise the third destructive wave.

"Slot your arrows!" she barked. "Mark your targets!"

In one unified movement, arrows were pulled from quivers, slotted to cords and longbows stretched and arched skywards. Barely had the next wave of boars cleared their four hundred fallen cronies than Bryony was yelling "fire!" and another two hundred raging beasts were cut down by the archers' deluge of death. The bodies of this last wave of rampaging beasts had fallen along the line that marked the start of the rain-soaked, mud-filled dip. The remaining four hundred bellowing boars trampled undeterred over the six hundred dead and maimed.

Poppy now brought her second strategy into play. She raised her left hand to halt the onslaught of her archers and allow the giant boars to progress. The beasts hit the dip. With surprised difficulty they were struggling to drag their legs through the mud that lurked beneath the deceiving shallow covering of last night's heavy rain. Finally, exhausted from their efforts, they reached the far side of the ditch. All that lay between them and the inviting gaps in the wooden stakes was a 300-metre stretch of no-man's-land. Stheno saw that an imminent breakthrough was at hand by the boars but also noted that their numbers were depleted by heavy losses from the arrow attack. She decided to launch her thousand screaming devils to boost the boars' ranks.

St. John saw another hawk turn to stone and fall at a spot where Stheno had now moved a little further up the centre of the field to urge on the charge of her demons. This marked the loss of his third bird. A reserve hawk fluttered up onto his forearm and he lovingly stroked it before sending it skywards to replace its dead comrade.

Poppy was keeping her nerve well. She had noted the launch of the demons but momentarily held the new threat in mental abeyance. Instead, she prioritised her focus on the boars. Poppy judged the remaining distance between the beasts and the gaps in the fortifications to have reached critical point. She raised her right arm high, let it hover there and then cut Athena's dagger sharply down to her side. This was the signal that Angelica had anxiously been anticipating. Up to this point she had waited patiently with her spearmen who were silently hiding along the tree line at the foot of the hill. When Poppy had first raised her arm, Angelica hovered in front of her troops and gave the order "stand to!" At this command, her men took one pace to the front and thrust their spears forward at the ready. The angel lifted her rallying- banner of Holly and red berries – the colours of her queen – and cried out:

"No ground will be given," she urged them. "Death before retreat!"

The spearmen roared their defiance. As Poppy cut her dagger arm sharply down, Angelica screamed out "charge!" to her soldiers and the spearmen burst out of the woods. The archers had already split their line to left and right at Poppy's signal and the troops had a clear run down to the gaps in the fortifications.

Poppy gave a sigh of relief as she watched the first part of her trap work with precision timing. The spearmen reached the gaps seconds before the boars and rammed the hilts of their spears into the ground. Going down on one knee they gripped the shafts with both hands and held the glinting steel tips steady at forty-five degree angles. The boars, in full gallop, suddenly had nowhere to go. In panic, they threw themselves to the left and right to avoid the clusters of bristling metal teeth, only to be impaled on the sharp wooden stakes either side of the spears. The boars that were following behind saw the spear-trap too late. Some were spiked in the throat and up through the base of the skull, while others, who tried to leap the blockade, were skewered through the guts.

Satisfied that the spearmen were able to hold the line, Poppy turned and nodded to Bryony. The White Archangel quickly reassembled her line of archers. Poppy watched the waves of devils carefully. They had already advanced one third of the way up the meadow. Again she raised her dagger and again the archers drew back their longbows. It took all her self-control to hold steady and let the thousand demons come screaming onwards. She kept thinking of King Henry V; he had been outnumbered by five-to-one, the same as she was. Like him, it would be the keeping of faith in her tactical ability and in the courage of her soldiers that would carry the day. The raging devils were now two-thirds of the way up the meadow. That was what Poppy had been waiting for because the narrowing tree line each side of the field had bunched the creatures much closer together now.

Poppy dropped her raised arm, Bryony yelled "fire" and the sky turned black with arrows again. However, this time, at Poppy's instructions, the leading and the second line of devils were left unscathed and it was two hundred of the creatures in the third wave that were cut down. Then, at Bryony's quick order, a further two hundred were cut down behind them by another deadly hail of arrows. This left a gap between the leading untouched four hundred and the last two hundred devils that were now trailing behind from having to struggle over the dead and dying. The demons that reached the wooden fortifications ran into chaos. Those boars that had not been impaled on wooden stakes were now trying to turn away from the lunging spears of the front line defenders. Despite their efforts to retreat, the boars were being pushed forward again by the onrushing charge of devils that had struggled through the muddy quagmire and lurched into them. The second wave of devils had waded into the muddy ditch but could not get out at the other side because of the jam of milling bodies in front of the stakes. Those devils, now marooned in the mud, started to sink up to their scab-ridden waists. They panicked and tried to retreat to whence they came but were blocked by the onrush of trailing devils that had finally caught them up.

Poppy now judged the time to be right for the next part of her plan. She pointed Athena's dagger towards her waiting herald. He immediately raised his bugle and trumpeted the personal signal that Poppy had allocated to Pig and Violetta. Snarling through bared teeth, the dogs burst out of the tree line on each side of the battlefield and led their howling packs into the fray. They raced to the rear of the muddy mire and attacked the last wave of devils to arrive from behind. The routine that Pig had given them to rehearse went into practice. The hounds split into units of three and while one menacingly circled the victim to distract its attention the other two went for the ankles. Sinking their teeth to the bone, the dogs unbalanced their quarry and felled them. The circling dog then pounced and sank its fangs into the throat. The ruse worked well but as would be expected in close-quarter combat, there were casualties and several dogs already lay dead or injured from the slicing tails of the demons and impaling horns.

Pig came up against one devil screaming in pain as it dragged one leg behind it. He managed to dodge the lashing tail that whipped past his head and leapt up to its throat. He sank his teeth into the creature's neck and squeezed his jaws together with all his might. Pig felt streaks of searing pain down his back as the devil's claws raked along his spine in an effort to throw him off. Relentlessly, Pig continued the pressure until the flow of blood that gushed from the demon's mouth had ceased and it collapsed to the ground dead. Only then did Pig see the cause of the devil's incapacitation; hanging from its ankle was a British Bulldog. The Bulldog was dead from a ripped-open rib cage but its jaws were still locked together in an unbreakable grip. Even in death, the Bulldog was still fighting on!

Pig's eyes searched the mayhem around him. He was desperately looking for Violetta and reassurance of her safety. He spotted her attacking a boar that had managed to drag itself out of the sucking mud and was making a staggering escape to the rear. Two of her Labrador bitches had the huge beast by its hind legs while Violetta clung resolutely to its bucking back and gnawed into the base of its skull. The boar faltered then collapsed to its knees like a pile of bricks. Pig smiled. "That's my girl," he thought. Content at seeing her, he raced off to urge on his own pack with blood-curdling howls.

The trap set by Poppy was, so far, going to plan. Her army had suffered losses. That was inevitable but in harsh military terms they were acceptable losses. Quickly, she took stock of the current situation:

The dogs were attacking and depleting the devils on the far side of the ditch. The boars and devils actually in the mire were engulfed up to the chest in mud and some were suffocating from the weight of those trying to claw their way out over the top of them. The boars that were being pressed up against the wooden stakes were gradually being killed or crippled by the constant jabbing of the spearmen. The boars and devils that were pushing up behind them were trapped in the no-man's-land between the fortifications and the mud mire. They rampaged back and forth with nowhere to go. At Poppy's signal, Bryony shouted orders to her archers and they started to pump arrows into the mass of scattering bodies in that area.

It was St. John who saw the threat first as he watched his spotter hawks. A fourth hawk had fallen from the sky at a spot that indicated Stheno was still placed centre field but had now moved forward a little more. The reason was soon apparent. "Aerial attack!" he yelled with urgency. Droning up the meadow, like a thousand-bomber raid, lumbered a swarm of gigantic black crows. They were slow and cumbersome but already they were a good way up the battlefield.

"Quick!" screamed Bryony to her archers. "Shoot them down now! Fire at will."

At three-quarters distance away, the archers had shot down two hundred. At halfway, they had shot down another two hundred. At the final quarter stage, the archers had downed a total of six hundred crows. Before another arrow could be slotted the remaining four hundred crows swooped down on them. Archers screamed in agony and staggered around blindly with gushing eye sockets where eyeballs had once been. A crow had one archer's head in a vice-like grip in its beak. As the vice tightened, the screams of the man did not hide the crunching collapse of his face and his teeth popping out one by one. Another archer lay writhing on the ground. The femoral artery, where a leg had been, continued pumping blood, which flew crazily into the air. The assailing crow still held the leg in its claws. The man's thrashing stopped as the crow skewered the exposed thigh bone of the leg stump into his guts.

Poppy started to vomit at the sight. Her mind went into a whirl. She had not catered for this! The archers were suffering unacceptable casualties with no way of defending themselves, yet she could not see a solution. Outnumbered by five to one, Poppy could not afford to incur such a loss without inflicting heavier losses in return. She looked around in desperation and then saw St. John running towards her. He was frantically waving to Bryony and Angelica to join him at the chariot. As he ran towards them, St. John skilfully side-stepped a swooping crow, parried its lunging beak with his shield and slit it open from gullet to tail with Athena's sword as it flashed overhead.

St. John needed to tell Poppy and the White Archangels his ad hoc plan. The inspiration had suddenly come to him from an ancient book by Plutarch. He had written a historical account on the ancient people of Sparta. The Spartans had a reputation for being tough, courageous and placing personal honour above all else. It was a few remembered lines from the book that had given St. John an idea. Plutarch had noted what a Spartan mother had said to her son as he made himself ready to go off to battle. She handed him his shield and said: "Either with this, or on this."

What she had done was spell out her expectations of him. There were only two ways that she was prepared to welcome his return home; either carrying his shield held high over his head in victory or being carried dead upon it. To come home alive but defeated was dishonourable and therefore not an option.

St. John hurriedly related his plan to the gathered trio. It was a desperate gamble. Like the Spartan mother's expectations of her son, there were to be no soft options. After they were all urgently apprised of St. John's idea, the group split up. However, that was not before the White Archangels had looped-the-loop to avoid swooping attacks, St. John had sliced the legs off an attacking crow and Poppy had thrown Athena's dagger to cut the head off another that had a nearby archer pinned to the ground.

Angelica flew off down to her spearmen at the fortification but while in mid-flight she was savaged by a diving crow. She crashed to the ground with a damaged wing. The crow screeched with vicious delight, aimed its beak at her eyes and hovered above Angelica for the kill. A shout of fear for their angel went up from her troops. Two spearmen gripped a shield at each end and another, with spear thrust skywards, ran forward to leap onto it. As his leading foot hit the shield, the other two heaved it upward with all their might. The running spearman was launched skywards and his spear pierced the guts of the crow as it descended upon the prostrate Angelica. The crow fell onto its back beside her, still straining its head around to jab its beak into her face. The shield bearers threw themselves forward to drop the shield on top of the embedded spear shaft, which was gyrating wildly as the crow thrashed from side to side. As they did so the third man leapt on top of it. His weight thrust the spear through the bird's backbone, into the ground and pinned it there. In a flash, he pulled out his dagger, jumped down onto the giant bird and decapitated it. Despite her pain, Angelica uttered her orders. The three spearmen gently lifted her onto an upturned shield, yelled for their comrades to rally to their angel and withdrew from the fortifications at breakneck speed back to the hill.

Bryony had returned to her archers and amid the chaos, organised them into small groups composed of two ranks. As they swung their mallets and spikes wildly in the air to try and fend off the aerial attack, the spearmen arrived. They split themselves into sections and stood at the sides and rear of the twin-ranked groups. Then they raised their shields high over the heads of the archers. The crows could no longer get at them. The birds that landed on top of the protective roof were skewered by the parting of shields and the upward thrust of spears. Crows that flew down and tried to attack at the sides were met with spears, mallets and daggers lunging out at them.

At the fortifications, those devils and giant boars that had been hung up on the wooden stakes or trapped in no-man's-land could not believe their luck. The fortifications were now deserted and Poppy was turning her chariot away to retreat up behind the shielded archers. The way was now wide open for a mass charge up the hill to the Golden Bluebell. With raging screams, bellows and snorts, they threw themselves forward in a dash. Poppy halted behind the archers. She grabbed a shield and spear from the chariot's armoury for protection from the danger above then nodded across to her herald. He immediately trumpeted out the personal signal of Pig and Violetta and blew the call for them to "return to your leader". The dogs broke off from the rear attack of the devils and boars, disappeared into the woods and reappeared at the base of the hill to gather around Poppy. She swept her spear across the flock of fluttering crows that were still desperately engaged in attacking the blocks of shielded archers and hissed a one-word order between gritted teeth: "Kill!"

A blood-curdling howl went up amongst the packs of dogs and bitches as they turned and bounded off. The crows were so engrossed in carrying out Stheno's order to destroy the archers that they never saw the pack coming. Again, the dogs and bitches of Pig and Violetta split into units of three. One of each unit sprang into the air at the hovering birds, snatched a dangling claw, brought it to the ground and the other two pounced to savage it. High pitched squawks of pain and mangled feathers flew through the air.

Amid the turmoil, St. John sorrowfully spotted another of his suicide hawks turn to stone and hurtle to the earth. That meant Stheno was still positioned in the middle of the battlefield but had moved a third of the way up the meadow and towards the trees on the left flank. It soon became apparent why. She had seen that her devils and giant boars were now pouring through the fortifications and up towards the base of the hill. Thinking the breakthrough had been made, she now launched her thousand fighting skeletons up the field in support.

Bryony, having seen the devils and boars negotiate the wooden stakes, turned to her archers. They were well protected by the overhead shields and were holding their two-rank formations below the metal canopies. "Slot your arrows and mark your targets," she yelled. "Front rank – fire!" The front rank let loose a horizontal swathe of arrows that thumped into the line of beasts breaking through. The front ranks of archers immediately dropped to one knee, pulling another arrow from their quivers to reload as they did so. This left a clear line of fire for the archers standing upright at the rear. "Rear rank – fire!" yelled Bryony. Another line of arrows winged at chest height across the field and thudded into the breaching monsters. At the command "front rank", the kneeling archers rose with longbows drawn, fired and dropped to one knee again, while the reloaded rear rank let fly. The precision bobbing manoeuvres by the archers flowed in unison with Bryony's one long machine-gun stream of orders. The frenzied charge of the beasts ground to a halt as the bodies started to pile up under the rapid sprays of arrows. Soon, they were starting to retreat back towards the fortifications. As this continued, the crows were being decimated from the thrusting spears and onslaught of the packs led by Pig and Violetta.

Poppy assessed that the remaining crows could be dealt with on a one-to-one combat basis or disabled by lightning attacks from the remaining nine reserve hawks that St. John now considered he could safely transfer to the task. Poppy decided that she need only give two more orders to seize and re-establish advantage at the fortifications before facing up to a new challenge of terror that had arisen. She signalled her herald and at her command he trumpeted the signal to the spearmen. Angelica, despite the pleas from her men, had refused to leave the battlefield. Still lying on the shield, she painfully gasped the command to her troops to break into line formation. At her order of "on guard," the men slung their shields on their left arm, gripped the shafts of their spears with both hands and thrust them forward. At her command of "advance", they trudged unrelentingly forwards toward the retreating enemy, the steel tips of their spears thrusting and lunging as they went.

In a blind rage at being repulsed, some beasts turned and threw themselves at the spearmen. One man had part of his cranium ripped away by the barb of a demon's slashing tail, leaving the pulsing pink jelly of his brain exposed. Another was screaming as a boar's tusks ripped open his stomach and his intestines were pulled out to trail across the mud. The boar triumphantly trampled on them. In his agony the pain-streaked eyes of the man stared at St. John in an appeal for salvation. St. John smashed his shield into the face of the boar then thrust Athena's sword into its throat. Knowing the man was going to die slowly and inevitably, all he could do was put him out of his pain. With tears flowing down his cheeks, he thrust the sword into the man's heart and finished his torment. St. John prayed that if a similar fate awaited him, someone would have the same courage to finish him off.

Shrieks continued around St. John from fatally-wounded boars and devils as the spearmen trudged relentlessly on. Screams also rent the air from those advancing soldiers that were having their ribs ripped open or limbs mangled. St. John tried to close his mind to their wailing pleas for help. "You must concentrate on Stheno!' his mind rebuked itself. Turning his back on his comrades, St. John withdrew. God, how he despised himself for it but his duty took priority over his personal feelings. This was what war was – the mangling of bodies and brutalising of souls.

At the herald's next fanfare, the dog packs broke and disappeared left and right into the woods. They reappeared on the far side of the muddy mire to resume their attack at the rear on the devils and giant boars being slowly pushed back by Angelica's spearmen.

Meanwhile, the lines of fighting skeletons had marched relentlessly up the field. The clatter of bones and banging of swords on shields in time with their steps brought a sound of terror to the dogs. Still savaging the retreating beasts, they were marooned on the wrong side of the fortification and totally exposed to attack at the rear from the advancing skeletons. Pig urged the pack to keep on attacking and trusted that Poppy would somehow protect them. She, in turn, had seen the danger and was ready for it. Poppy nodded to her ever-watching herald and he sounded out a signal to Bryony. Immediately she yelled orders to her archers and they split left and right to clear the assembly area. At another blast from the herald's bugle, the men-at-arms trudged out of hiding from the trees at the foot of Honeypot Hill and down towards the fortifications. Poppy steered Xanthus and Balius to take her place at their head. She drew Athena's dagger, shouted "home!" and threw it. The dagger winged its way over the spearmen and the fortifications. The blade and jewels in its handle glinted in the sunlight. At that signal, a group of spearmen yanked a clump of wooden stakes out of the ground in the centre of the wall. Poppy called to her horses and the chariot careered down towards the gap.

Athena's dagger continued its flight and thudded into the earth in front of the Ground Ivy that had been planted before the battle started. The dagger spun with a whirl of blue in the soil. At that signal, the Ground Ivy shook and then propagated with lightning speed to burst across the mud ditch in an unstoppable raft of thick, matted roots. Athena's dagger returned 'home' to Poppy's outstretched hand as her chariot ploughed through the gap and onto the carpet of racing Ground Ivy. Any marauding beasts that got in the way were cut down by the spinning scythes on Poppy's chariot wheels. The men-at-arms poured through the corridor after her to the open meadow. Behind them, retreating beasts were wallowing in the quagmire of mud, while being speared from the front or savaged at the rear by the dogs.

Once on firm ground, Poppy brought the chariot to a halt and threw her arms out wide in a signal to her fighters. The two hundred men-at-arms responded by fanning out behind her in a thin line across the field and standing rigid.

The fighting skeletons continued to advance towards Poppy's meagre line of resistance with a clattering stomp. The black hollows of their eye sockets seemed lifeless, yet their gaping jawbones and exposed teeth gave the impression that they were laughing at her defiance. Poppy raised her arm, Bryony called to her archers and the rows of longbows were drawn back and upwards at full stretch. Poppy brought her arm sharply down to her side. Once more the sky turned black over her head as the arrows fanned across the field. The rain of death fell on the battlefield and the splintering impact was accompanied by the crackling sound of splitting bones. Swords and shields fell to the ground as radiuses, ulnae and clavicles were shattered. Some skeletons, with a femur sheered at the pelvis, were scooting around on the ground in circles. The rest marched on indifferently. When the distance between the skeletons and Poppy became too close to guarantee her safety from the arrows, Bryony stopped her archers' volleys of destruction.

As soon as the arrows ceased falling, Poppy screamed out with vengeance to the men-at-arms: "No prisoners! Kill them all!" Poppy's venomous outburst stemmed from her memory of the 'Arena of Death'. With eyes blazing in rage, she snapped at the reins of her horses, yelled "come on then!" to her men and the chariot lunged forward. She veered right and ran along between the two leading ranks of skeletons. Bones were flying everywhere as the scythes on the wheels cut the skeletons down like skittles and Poppy's wildly swinging sword lopped off skulls. Two rib cages flew over her head from the tossing spikes of Xanthus and Balius. Then her men-at-arms were in among the skeletons. Their tway-blades whirled like murderous windmills. Their long knives parried skeleton attacks as their broadswords split sternums and ribs asunder, severed spines and hacked off femurs. Some men-at-arms sheathed their long knives to grasp their heavy swords with both hands in downward swings that sliced through skeleton helmets and cleaved skulls in two. Others replaced lost daggers with maces, content to take enemy blows to their heavy armour so that they could smash the spiked metal balls into bony faces, whilst driving and twisting swords into ribcages

As Poppy spun her chariot around for a second run down the lines of the enemy, a skeleton leapt onto the back of Balius. Bony fingers gripped his mane to yank the head back and the other arm came up to thrust a sword into the horse's throat. Poppy drew Athena's dagger, threw it and screamed "cut and home!" In one continuous movement, the blade severed the arm of the descending sword. It cut off the skull and hacked through both hip joints so that the legs gripping the horse's flanks fell away and the remaining rib cage went bouncing under the chariot wheels to be pulverised to powder. Athena's dagger zipped back into Poppy's outstretched hand as she fired up her rampaging steeds to commence a second run of annihilation.

Stheno was shocked to see that her fighting skeletons were not faring well at the hands of this slip-of-a-girl and her hacking, wielding, men-at-arms. Those of the armour-plated human battle-tanks that had lost broadswords in combat had now replaced them with spiked metal balls on long chains. They swung them above their heads to crush and scatter skulls like coconuts. The bones of these headless frames, which staggered blindly around the battlefield, were being scattered to the four winds by the spinning scythes of Poppy's hurtling chariot and the spikes and flaying hooves of her horses. In desperation, Stheno launched her deadly blood-sucking creatures of the night to reinforce her depleted fighting skeletons. As she did so, St. John saw another of his brave spotter hawks turn to stone and fall to the ground. It indicated that Stheno had moved completely over to the left flank to hide at the edge of the tree line.

At no time during the battle had Stheno ever attempted to move further forward than she already was. Logically, Stheno could have strolled up the battlefield unopposed, because every living creature that stood in her way would be turned into a pillar of stone. There was only one thing that had held her back; the fear of a stray arrow. The arrow was not a living thing that could be turned to stone. It was a wooden-shafted, armour-piercing, flesh-tearing, bone-shattering, steel-tipped missile that harboured neither conscience nor showed fear or favour. Stheno had no answer to it. St. John saw another hawk go down. The position of its fall informed him that Stheno had remained hidden just inside the edge of the tree line but was now moving along it and up the battlefield towards Honeypot Hill. This way, St. John concluded, she could urge on her gruesome army and be near to the Golden Bluebell when her creatures finally seized it for her. More importantly, for her own safety, she was removed from the danger of any stray arrows.

CHAPTER 11
St. John Makes His Move

St. John set off with Athena's sword and shield into the woods on the left flank. He too picked his way along the tree line to wait for her. Halfway down the length of the meadow he spotted a particular tree. The thick girth of its trunk was ideal to hide behind. It was also at the edge of the wood, so he had a good view of the battlefield. There was also a personal reason for his choice and St. John made it with deliberation and solemnity. His choice was an English Oak and he chose it in memory of his mother and the stories from history that she used to tell him and Poppy at bedtime. Wherever possible she would centre her historic tales on wild flowers and trees. St. John's mind drifted back to that night by the fireside when mum sat back with a bag of salt and vinegar crisps (she was a pushover for them) and said: "Ah, yes, the English Oak."

Mum had related the tale of this great tree. It was, by tradition, the national tree of England. In past centuries the English Oak had been associated with shipbuilding and, in particular, the fleets of naval warships which became known as England's 'wooden walls'. Mum had gone on to tell how England's wellbeing had been under threat from the combined fleets of France and Spain. The struggle for sea supremacy came to a head at the Battle of Trafalgar when Horatio Nelson led the English fleet in his flagship, H.M.S. Victory, against them. Despite being heavily outnumbered, Nelson drove his ship into the enemy and engaged several enemy vessels at once. Nelson was renowned for leading from the front and during the battle, whilst striding the deck and instilling his sailors with exceptional courage, he was mortally wounded by a sniper's bullet from an enemy ship at close quarters. He was carried below the Oak deck and as he lay dying under its shroud, he was told that the enemy fleet had been cut to ribbons. A great and decisive victory had been won. St. John's highly charged emotions led him to feel that if he was to die in his encounter with Stheno then he would prefer to die shrouded under English Oak as Nelson had done.

St. John pressed his back to the Oak tree and seemed to feel a gentle wave of calming strength flow through his body. Was it from the echoes of the English Oak's glorious past feats in history, or from the tree's resident Dryad nymph, or was it just his imagination? He would never know. He thrust Athena's sword into the ground, close and slightly hidden behind his right thigh and clasped her polished bronze shield in front of him. St. John looked across the field to the fortification. He could see the dog packs of Pig and Violetta and Angelica's spearmen still ripping into the dwindling devils and boars. The last of the crows were fluttering around in a last-ditch attempt to inflict injuries on the archers. However, their efforts were being harried too much to be effectual. Every time they regrouped to make a concerted attack, the remaining hawks that St. John had released from their spotter duties split the crows apart with streaking dives out of the sun – like Spitfires attacking lumbering bombers. Wings were being shattered, tails torn off and groups of the black menace spiralled to the ground to crash in piles of mangled wreckage. Pig and Violetta were frenziedly bounding up and down with teeth bared to urge their hounds on in their savagery. The injured Angelica, still being carried on a shield, strained up on one elbow to give directions to her spearmen and Bryony was flitting back and forth behind her archers. Every time she waved her arms, another hail of arrows shot skywards and splattered the battlefield.

As the arrows passed overhead to reach the advancing blood-suckers, St. John looked down to see his sister below. Bones were flying everywhere as she marauded through the thick of the fighting skeletons with her chariot and raging horses. He felt a surge of admiration as he watched her in action. She threw Athena's dagger to slice off the skull of a skeleton that had pinned one of her men to the ground, while at the same time heaving her shield-bearing arm up and out to smash a skeleton full in the face as it tried to clamber aboard her chariot. In one swift movement, she thrust out her hand, retrieved the returning dagger, sheathed it, drew Xanthus and Balius to a swerving halt, leaned over to pull the man-at-arms upright and then plunged back into the fray again. "Was this the quiet, polite, considerate young woman who had been pushed around at school for being just that?" thought St. John. "Yes, dad was right. The big-mouthed bullies act the way they do to hide the truth about themselves; inside they are cowards! The true warriors were the Poppys of this world; the ones that quietly got on with life, yet constantly overcame their daily self-doubt and fears to meet the real challenges of everyday living."

St. John's eyes refocused on the arrows that had passed over the battling Poppy and watched them descend into the hordes of blood-suckers that were rushing up the meadow to bolster the flagging ranks of the skeletons. The striking arrows brought forth screams of pain and sprays of thin, pink puss from their quivering bodies. The more St. John saw Bryony jumping up and down waving her arms, the more intense became the hail of death. Again, as the blood-suckers drew close to Poppy and the arrows posed a danger to Bryony's beloved leader, the White Archangel's arms shot up and the arrows ceased.

As the last arrow sliced its spurting course through the guts of a charging blood-sucker, Poppy swept her arm up to launch Athena's dagger skywards. The glittering sapphires of its handle sparkled in the sunlight as the dagger spun in mid-air. The watchful herald instantly trumpeted the personal signal of Sorrel.

She had suffered much anguish and impatience as she waited with her knights in the woods. When things had seemed to be going badly at the fortifications it took all her powers of command and authority to stop her knights from charging out to help – and thus giving away the element of surprise. The only thing that had held them back was unshakeable faith in Poppy's judgement and total obedience to her orders as their leader.

Now it was the turn of the knights to exact revenge. Sorrel took the wooden staff, wreathed with Holly and red berries that she had woven earlier and hoisted it high. "For our queen, Mother Nature, and for our leader, Poppy!" yelled Sorrel. "Victory or death!" As she plunged out onto one side of the battlefield with her cohort of knights, the second cohort burst out of the woods on the other.

The galloping horses pounded unnoticed along the back line of blood-suckers who were pushing up behind the fighting skeletons. When the knights met in the middle of the battlefield, Sorrel gave the command and they turned inwards to attack the blood-suckers from the rear. Amid the yells and clashing steel of battle, wails and screams rose up from the vile creatures as two hundred lances thrust through their bodies. The knights disengaged, pulled back, regrouped in line and at Sorrel's command they charged again. As the blood-suckers turned in surprise to see what had hit them, another two hundred were lanced through by the knights' second charge. Recovering from the shock, some of the creatures leapt upon the knights as they disengaged for a third charge. Horses were pulled down and fangs sunk into their throats. Knights were dragged to the ground, visors on helmets ripped open and flabby lips closed over the openings for teeth to sink into their faces. Bits of lungs and stomach were drawn up through the screaming knights' throats as the creatures sucked the life's blood from their bodies.

Poppy, despite being in the thick of the fighting, had constantly kept her eye on the flow of battle. She now assessed that the situation at the fortification was well under control. The archers, with daggers, spikes and mallets, had moved forward to reinforce the spearmen. The dogs could now be spared from the fight. She gave a signal to her herald and he trumpeted out the call for Pig and Violetta to "return to your leader". The packs broke off from their engagement with the boars and devils and ran down the field to rally to Poppy. She then directed them to skirt the battle-line of the skeletons and come up behind the blood-suckers to assist the knights. As the dogs pounded off to do her bidding, Pig slipped away from them unnoticed. His mind was not now reacting to the mayhem around him. His brain was impervious to the shouts and screams of battle, the clash of steel and the spurting of blood. Pig's life did not matter anymore. His whole being was now focused on one thing – the ultimate act of betrayal!

Stealthily, Pig returned to the rear of Poppy unseen. Everyone around her was engaged in hand-to-hand combat and fighting for their lives. Instinct told him that if Poppy was to be treacherously disposed of then this was the right time. No one was in a position to see any danger coming. She could be struck down and nobody would be the wiser. He crept closer to her chariot, lay down, half hidden by the mutilated body of a man-at-arms and waited for the moment of opportunity that must surely arise.

CHAPTER 12
St. John and Stheno

The unending wait to meet his fate had unnerved St. John. He pressed his back into the English Oak tree until it hurt in an effort to stop the uncontrollable shaking of his body from the fear of anticipation. Gradually, to his relief, the trembling in his arms and legs ceased. However, a further trembling started, which brought a cold sweat to his forehead. The trembling was not from his body - it was from Athena's sword. Perseus had informed him that having been imbrued with the blood of Medusa, the sword would sense the close presence of any Gorgon thereafter. Stheno was coming! The increasing tremors from the sword, as it stood thrust in the ground behind his right thigh, told St. John that she was getting nearer and nearer. Feverishly, his mind went through the strike routine with the sword that he had practised again and again in what seemed an eternity ago.

Then a voice sounded that stopped his racing thoughts in their tracks. The wonderful voice made his heart leap with joy. In the next instant it had his mind silently screaming with excruciating anguish! St. John's straining ears heard the voice of his mother call out across the battlefield: "Poppy! Poppy! I am hurt. Please help me. Please help your mother." Stheno's imitation was playing the most vicious trick of all. She was using the vulnerability of the girl's love for her dead mother to kill Poppy and there was nothing St. John could do about it! The voice of betrayal drifted tantalisingly across the battlefield. He saw his sister straining up

93

on her tiptoes in the chariot and frantically casting her eyes over the turmoil that was going on around her.

St. John desperately wanted to shout out to her: "For God's sake don't look Poppy, she'll kill you!" Yet, if he did so, he would give away his position and he would die. Frantically his brain ran through the options. If Poppy was going to die there was nothing he could do about it. If he tried to warn her, they would both die. If he died there would be nothing to keep Stheno from seizing the golden Bluebell and destroying all wild flowers and the Earth itself. His duty to protect the planet superseded the safety of his sister. His crushing conclusion was that he had no choice but to do nothing and accept the death of Poppy.

Stheno's repugnant imitation of their mother's voice continued calling to Poppy and the girl kept frantically casting around to locate it. All this time Stheno was getting closer to St. John's tree. He could now hear the hissing of the vipers writhing from her head and the clanking together of her brass hands. "Just one more step and she will be level with the Oak," he thought. "Please, please, Poppy - don't find us now. Just give me one more second." Too late! He saw her face turn towards them. She was his sister but she was his dead sister now.

One more step took Stheno level with the Oak. Somewhere in the mind that was numbed by the death of Poppy the mechanism of St. John's survival instinct clicked into place and his brain screamed: "Now!" He shot his arms out to the left and rammed Athena's polished shield into the ground then slammed his back against the Oak tree again. There, he remained perfectly still with arms straight down by his side. His body stayed rigid but his right hand furtively crept around the back of his thigh to clasp the hidden handle of Athena's vibrating sword. The positioned angle of the shield was perfect; he could see everything. Perseus' description of the Gorgon sisters had prepared St. John for what he would see but it had not prepared him for the nauseous waves of revulsion that raked his stomach from the reflected image that the shining shield now showed him. Stheno's hair was entwined with a thousand writhing, hissing vipers. Her protruding teeth were as long as the tusks of a boar and her cold, lifeless, brass hands swung back and forth across the slime-scaled skin of a lizard-like body. In that moment, as they stared at each other in the reflection of the shield, time seemed to stand still and the world stopped turning. St. John struggled to keep from vomiting, whilst Stheno assimilated the image of this defenceless, frightened youth who was pressed against the tree in fear. This was the brother of the stupid girl that had caused Stheno so much trouble and now he was going to die for it.

Despite the repulsive sight, St. John searched the Gorgon's face for any sign that might signal the moment of Stheno's attack. It came in the form of a narrowing of her bloodshot eyes as she raised a clawed foot to step around the tree. In that instant, St. John's left arm moved across his body and its hand joined that of his other on the hilt of the sword. With gritted teeth and every bit of strength he could muster from his stress-ridden body, he heaved Athena's sword upwards and outwards in a wide arc. All the bewilderment, loss, loneliness, grieving, loathing, hate and anger that raged within him at the death of Poppy boiled up like a cauldron in his chest.

As the sword winged along its path of destiny, his clenched teeth parted and the howl of the savage beast, that lies within us all, rent the air: "Die you bastaaaard!" There was a thud and a shuddering up St. John's arms as the sword cut through Stheno's throat, smashed the larynx, sliced the carotid arteries and severed the spine at the base of her skull. Her head flew off. There was a second of silence, punctured only by the gurgling sounds of pumping blood from her gaping neck. The forward impetus of Stheno's stride brought her decapitated body from around the tree to crash at his feet. St. John screwed his eyes shut, lest her head should follow.

Still keeping his eyes tightly shut he went down on his hands and knees and started to grope around for the offending head. His fingers found a trail of stiff grass. The blades were matted together with thick, warm goo. Gibbering out words of self-encouragement to overcome his disgust, his fingers traced along the sticky trail. The next thing he knew, he was retching and vomiting uncontrollably as his searching hand found a gaping hole and entered the stinking red jam pot that was her skull. When he had emptied his stomach of everything except its lining, he pushed the head into a goatskin bag that Perseus had given him for the purpose.

As he rammed the head home, an eyeball popped out of its socket and into his hand. The Gorgon's head was now dead and the eye had slowly died along with it. As it had done so, the inner vitreous humour and the slimy secretion of mucus that covered its outer surface, gradually crystallised and turned the eye to glass. Delphyne had once told St. John about the circumstances of his capture by Medusa and how just the sighting of one of her eyes had been enough to temporarily paralyse the dragon in his tracks. St. John thought that Stheno's eyeball might be a useful item to him in the future and so he stuffed it in a pocket of his tunic. He pulled the drawstrings tight on the goatskin bag and knotted them several times.

Only now did St. John fall on his back and allow his tired body to collapse. Slowly, he opened his eyes. A beautiful sight greeted him. It was the sunlight filtering down through the broad green leaves of the English Oak tree that seemed to tower over him like a protective gentle giant. His thoughts strayed again to his mother and her stories from history. He remembered the last dying words his mum retold to him that had been spoken by Horatio Nelson as he lay under the English Oak deck of H.M.S. Victory: "God and my country". The words held the same meaning for St. John at this moment but there was now more to his triumph than that; his victory was for his dead sister, Poppy.

The thought of his sister roused him back into action. He moved out of the tree line onto the meadowland and caught the stray horse of a slaughtered knight. He removed its bridle and reins and used them to tie the ankles of Stheno's body. St. John attached the other ends to the saddle then slapped the horse's back and sent it galloping. The horse wildly pounded around the battlefield with Stheno's headless body bumping and banging from side to side as it was dragged along the ground behind. St. John hitched the goatskin bag to his belt, sheathed Athena's sword and slung her shield on his back. He saw Poppy's chariot, still motionless, in the middle of the meadow and headed in that direction. As he trudged towards it the cheers rang in his ears when Poppy's army saw the headless body of their deadly enemy being humiliatingly dragged up and down. With Stheno dead and their objective lost, the remnants of her evil army were giving up the fight. Mass groups were being herded together at sword point in dejected surrender. All the planning, sacrifice, blood, sweat and tears had finally paid off and brought about a great victory but for St. John it had no meaning any more. He should have been elated but his only thought was: "I'm so damned tired that even the moment of triumph seems just a part of the same bad nightmare."

As he neared Poppy's chariot, he saw the bowed heads of Xanthus and Balius. On the far side of it he could see Angelica, Bryony and Sorrel gathered around in a huddle, staring down. Silent tears rolled down their cheeks. A line of dogs circled the scene and sat with heads back, softly howling to the sky. Pig was nowhere to be seen. The horses became skittish and as they restlessly moved around, the chariot rolled forward. St. John saw the body of Poppy lying full length on the ground.

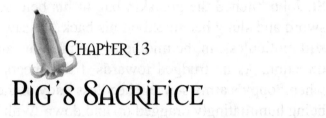

CHAPTER 13
PIG'S SACRIFICE

St. John's mind had ceased to fully function since he had allowed himself to collapse in relief under the Oak tree after the killing of Stheno. Yet, even in its dulled state, a small detail in the tragic picture before his blurred eyes was nagging at him. It was the scratches. Yes. That's it. It was the scratches on Poppy's neck. They were bleeding! The old saying 'you can't get blood out of a stone' began to register in his tired mind. The figure of Poppy was not grey like stone. Furthermore, it was not rigid like stone. In fact, the shoulders were shaking in short convulsive movements. As St. John ran forwards he could hear her sobbing. "Poppy, you're alive!" he yelled in relief. "But I thought you were dead."

She looked at him incredulously. "No. I'm not dead. Why should you think that? It is my wonderful friend who is dead," she wailed. St. John then saw the reason why Poppy was lying stretched on the ground. She was cradling the stone remains of Pig's body in her arms. Violetta was licking at his stone-cold cheek.

Between sobs, Poppy told St. John what had happened. Embroiled in the heat and noise of battle, she thought she heard her mother calling to her. At first, Poppy thought it was her imagination. Then she was convinced she heard it again and thought, by some miracle, that the gods had sent mum to help her. Amid all the shouts and cries it was difficult to identify where it was coming from. Poppy had looked almost everywhere around the battlefield and seen nothing. Then another plea for help from her mother drifted through the chaos. It seemed to come from Poppy's left. She turned to look towards the tree line and suddenly a black streak shot across her face to momentarily block her view. As the black streak passed her, the back legs of the leaping Pig kicked out, catching her on the neck and sending her toppling backwards. It was his claws that had caused the scratches to her neck. As Poppy fell backwards into the chariot, she had seen Pig go over the side with a thud. When she had finally recovered her breath from the impact Poppy dragged herself up to see St. John across the field, head bowed, slumped against an Oak tree and leaning on his sword. Then she had looked down and seen the block of stone that was Pig, lying against the chariot wheel. Poppy had no idea of how it had occurred or what had really happened.

Only when St. John explained to her what he had seen take place did his sister fully realise how close to death she had been and how Pig had selflessly given his life to save hers. Knowing it meant certain death, Pig had looked upon Stheno to ensure the line of his body would block Poppy's own eyes from staring death in the face. She was alive because of his sacrifice. The death of Pig had been painful enough for Poppy but the realisation that he had died to save her was almost unbearable. Her sobs became uncontrollable as she clung to the block of stone in her arms. Violetta nuzzled up to Poppy and also whined out her sense of loss.

Whilst St. John comforted her, the White Archangels gently lifted Pig's body into the chariot. Led by Poppy, the solemn parade slowly wended its way back to the fortifications. St. John remained behind to deal with the aftermath on the battlefield. He tried to ignore the absolute slaughter of the 'Beasts from Hell' that were piled around him. However, even in his state of anger against them, it was difficult to do. His mum and dad had always brought him up to respect life and the right to the existence of others, regardless of how base he thought them to be. When he now forced himself to consider the monsters from a philosophical point of view, he could begrudgingly accept that it was not personally their fault. They had been created like that and knew no better. The real guilt and responsibility lay with those who had spawned and raised them – Medusa and Hecate. Regardless of these thoughts, St. John had to prioritise and see to the needs of his own men first.

What St. John found was a situation almost too horrendous to contemplate. The mangled, bleeding bodies of injured knights, dogs, spearmen and men-at-arms lay scattered everywhere. Now the noise of battle had ceased, the silence only served to magnify the groans of pain and pitiful cries for help that rang in his ears. Horses with deep gashes to their flanks, or broken legs, whinnied out their suffering as they lay struggling on the ground to get up. Elsewhere, the soldiers of Poppy's army and the creatures of Stheno's horde that died in the battle had returned back to their original wild flower form and lay withered and dead amid the grass and mud. There was nothing he could do for them. Assuming responsibility of command, St. John stifled his own feelings of mourning, switched to automaton mode, gave orders and organised groups to guard the prisoners and comfort the injured. One duty that he personally took upon himself was to bury the headless body of Stheno. The vision of it being dragged up and down the battlefield by a stampeding horse had brought satisfaction to his heart. Now, after the death of Pig, it offended his sight.

When he had done all he could, St. John trudged back to the fortifications to inform Poppy. She had also regained some of her composure and like St. John, was automatically going through the motions of organising the archers to aid her injured men at the defences and remove the wooden stakes. The twin brother and sister then sat down with the three White Archangels to discuss the current situation. The Golden Bluebell had been saved and the beauty of the Earth would safely continue for the benefit and pleasure of mankind and all living things. However, several problems remained. Everything that had taken place had to be kept as secret as possible. If this ever got out, every greedy person and megalomaniac in the world would descend upon Honeypot Hill to seek the Golden Bluebell and steal its power.

So, what should they do now with the remainder of the captured evil creatures? They could not release them to wreak havoc in the world but there was nowhere secluded and secure enough to imprison them. If these creatures ever fell into the hands of corrupt individuals, or regimes, they would misuse them for their own evil purposes. The only solution was to slaughter them all in cold blood. It was not a task that St. John, or any of the others, relished having to execute. Also, what should they do with the injured and the remainder of Poppy's army? Thanks to Flos, Poppy had been given the means to turn the wild flowers into real beings that she needed for her cause. Now, she had no means of turning them back into wild flowers again! So, how did they propose to keep the existence of the Golden Bluebell a secret from the world when all these things existed that would cause awkward questions to be asked? The Government and the public would tend to notice the odd man-eating monster hanging around on street corners or mediaeval armies marching up and down the motorways. While the 'peace council' of five tossed around possible solutions (none of which were feasible in the slightest) they were distracted by excited shouts from the battlefield. When they looked, they saw all the soldiers with their heads strained back and pointing upwards.

CHAPTER 14

MOTHER NATURE

From the depths of the azure sky a white dot had appeared. As it slowly drew closer and larger, Poppy and St. John could see wings – long, graceful wings.

"What is that?" frowned Poppy as she turned to enquire of the three White Archangels. She was talking to herself. Angelica, Bryony and Sorrel were already flitting down the meadow and babbling to each other in high-pitched tinkles of excitement. Within moments, the fit and able-bodied soldiers had followed the angels. Even the injured were hopping and crawling after them as best they could. The pair stood alone to curiously watch the shining white object descend to Earth. As it glided towards the centre of the meadow they could see the outline to which the gracefully flapping wings were attached. They sprouted from a huge white horse.

"It's Pegasus!" yelled St. John. "And that's got to be the goddess Mother Nature that he's got on his back. Andromeda must have pleaded a case to Zeus for a 'Second Coming' to have Pegasus fetch Mother Nature and bring her back to Earth."

"But why didn't she tell us that she intended to do that?" asked Poppy in a confused voice. "Have the deaths of all these good wild flowers been in vain?"

"Don't forget that Andromeda is an immortal, not a goddess" pointed out St. John. "There's no way that she could guarantee influencing Zeus to issue such a major command – not even with Hera backing her up! Neither could she assume that Mother Nature would arrive in time to stop Stheno. As for us, we're just mere mortals. The best any god, goddess, or immortal would have expected of us is some sort of 'holding action' until Mother Nature relieved us. They wouldn't have expected total victory but they forgot they were dealing with Poppy Flos – stubborn descendant of Flos the Flower Girl!" He smiled at Poppy's obvious embarrassment.

Pegasus gave a last sweep of his wings and gently landed on the battlefield. Mother Nature was sitting astride his broad back. She was indeed everything that Electra had described to St. John. Her fair hair radiated like golden sunbeams around her delicate face and her slight figure was adorned from top to toe in beautiful wild flowers. The soft flowing gown that she wore was made of pale yellow Evening Primrose, woven together with Silver Weed. The slender feet were encased in the softest Bluebells, whilst her tiny hands were warmed by purple Foxgloves. Around her neck hung a necklace of pink Water-plantains and her earrings were tiny blue Speedwell flowers that matched the colour of her eyes. Mother Nature's glory was the crown of deep green Holly and bright red berries that she wore on her head. The heady perfume of every wild flower in the universe drifted around her. Silver stardust snorted from the nostrils of Pegasus as he meekly knelt down and the goddess gracefully stepped to the ground. As she leaned forward to do so, Buttercup petals showered from her golden locks. Every soldier in the army of wild flowers went down on one knee across the battlefield to pay homage to their queen.

Angelica, Bryony and Sorrel hovered before her and bowed. Mother Nature placed a loving hand on the head of each in fondness. Poppy watched the White Archangels go into deep conversation with their queen. There was much waving of arms and pointing here and there across the meadow as they retold the events of what had happened. Then Poppy saw them turn and point to both her and St. John. Mother Nature looked up and gave the pair a smile of approval. With that, she held out her hand and Pegasus moved alongside her and knelt down. She gracefully slid onto his back again and with a beat of his wings, they glided low over the field of battle.

Clutching his mane with her left hand, Mother Nature leaned out over the neck of Pegasus and swept her right hand to and fro. She returned the surviving monsters of evil to the original wild flowers that they had once been. Catching some of the silver stardust from the snorting nostrils of Pegasus, she scattered it over the flowers of evil and cast a spell that bound them within nature's world of beauty and purity forever. For the injured and dying of her own good wild flowers, she swept her arm over the soldiers as Pegasus circled the meadowland. Their injuries were instantly healed and they were restored to health. Mother Nature could do nothing for those of Poppy's warriors that had died and now lay scattered as withered wild flowers across the field. To ensure that their sacrifice would be remembered until the end of time she planted a Forget-me-not at every spot where one had fallen in battle.

Poppy and St. John watched in awe as Mother Nature finished weaving her magic. Pegasus then landed at the bottom of the meadow. There he began to slowly walk up the avenue formed by flanking lines of soldiers and horses, which stretched up to the foot of Honeypot Hill where Poppy and St. John stood motionless. As the flying horse passed by, each guard of honour knelt to their queen. Soon the magical horse halted in front of the brother and sister and knelt before them. Mother Nature dismounted and accompanied by the smiling White Archangels she approached the pair. Unsure of the focus of attention they had become, Poppy curtsied awkwardly and St. John gave a hurried bow. Mother Nature addressed the pair in a soft, lilting voice:

"My White Archangels have told me everything about you. They have informed me of your ancestral history, the death of your mother and the risks you have now taken with your own lives to protect the creations of my realm. You are truly Children of the Stars."

Before the pair had a chance to voice their unworthiness at such a compliment from a goddess, she turned to Angelica, who held out a toadstool. Mother Nature passed her hand over it and it was transformed into a red velvet stool. Angelica placed it before Poppy and with a reassuring smile indicated that she should kneel upon it. Dumbfounded, Poppy knelt without protest. Bryony then handed Mother Nature a linked string of bright yellow Buttercups and a single Bluebell.

The goddess passed her hand over the wild flowers to transform them into a thick gold chain from which hung a tiny golden Bluebell.

"This Bluebell is the mark of your authority and is symbolic of the power I will bestow upon you over the flora on Earth and in the universe," she stated.

She drew Athena's dagger from the sheath at Poppy's side and held it up.

"By the wish and command of Athena and in the spirit of the special friendship between herself, Andromeda and Flos, this dagger is given to you to keep."

Mother Nature passed her hand over the weapon and it was transformed into a gold miniature of the same dagger. The goddess leaned forward and whispered in Poppy's ear: "Athena instructs me to tell you that, whenever you need it, just touch the gold emblem and her dagger will appear and disappear in your hand at your bidding."

With that, she attached it on the chain next to the golden Bluebell and placed it around Poppy's neck. Then Sorrel stepped forward and held out a single sprig of Holly. The goddess passed her hand over it and the twig instantly wove itself into a crown.

As Sorrel slowly lowered the crown onto Poppy's head, Mother Nature closed her eyes, lifted her face to the heavens and said:

"In the name of The Great One and by my own wish, I decree that this young woman, known as Poppy Flos, shall reign over my realm on Earth as Princess of Wild Flowers. This status demands a duty of allegiance to Poppy from the entire flora on the planet and she shall possess special powers that I now bestow upon her."

With that, the goddess took Poppy's hands in hers and as she knelt there, the girl felt a tremendous surge of power run from her fingers, up her arms and through her entire body. Poppy almost fainted from the magic that swept through her and as she closed her eyes at the sensation, a million different shapes and colours of wild flowers spun across the inner vision of her mind and a thousand different perfumes invaded her nostrils. Just as suddenly, the surge had gone and the angels were helping her to her feet.

Angelica ushered St. John to kneel on the stool. Mother Nature took Athena's sword. Touching both his shoulders with the blade, she declared:

"I dub you Knight Protector. You shall defend my realm."

Angelica then held out to Mother Nature a single yellow Coltsfoot flower and a linked string of bright yellow Buttercups. She passed a hand over them and they were transformed into a thick gold chain with the gold miniature of a winged horse attached. She pointed to it and said:

"Touch the emblem of the winged horse and he will magically appear to serve you. His name is Gaspeus and he will fly you wherever you wish to go. The emblem also symbolises your status as Knight Protector." The goddess then laid the sword and shield of Athena in front of him and said:

"In the eyes of Athena, you have proved yourself a worthy warrior with the slaying of Stheno. By her wish and command, these are given to you."

Mother Nature passed her hand over them and they were transformed into gold miniatures which she attached to his chain of office and placed around his neck. She quietly whispered in

St. John's ear: "Athena instructs me to say that whenever you need them, just touch the gold emblems and they will appear and disappear in your hands at your bidding." Sorrel solemnly lowered a crown of Holly on his head.

At the conclusion of the ceremony, Mother Nature took both young people to the chariot where the stone effigy of Pig still lay. She saw the tears welling up in their eyes again.

"Do not be sad my Children of the Stars," soothed the goddess. "Athena is a daughter of Zeus and holds his affection. He also owes me many favours and will have little choice but to sanction what we both do now."

She raised her arms to the sky and called out the name of Athena. Immediately, a bolt of electric blue lightning hurtled down from the heavens and the body of Pig vanished before their eyes.

"There, it is done," said the goddess. "He is immortalised. Look to the heavens tonight and you will see a tiny new star in the constellation of Canis Major, the 'Great Dog'. He will be Pig's companion and together they will be free to roam the universe and hunt with the great Orion."

Poppy turned to the goddess and hesitantly asked: "You have shown us gratitude and honoured us beyond our wildest dreams but please may I beg one more favour from you? It's not really for us that I ask. It is for Aunt Kay and Pig himself, who I know had strong feelings for Violetta. I wondered if you might.......?"

Mother Nature raised her hand to halt Poppy's embarrassment, smiled and said: "Yes. You may keep Violetta. She has already spoken to me and asked for permission to stay with you. I give her to you as a fivefold gift. Now, you must both mount the chariot and take to the field. Your army waits to greet their triumphant Princess of Wildflowers and Knight Protector."

They climbed aboard and Violetta jumped up after them. With a gentle slap of the reins Poppy set Xanthus and Balius off at a gentle canter down the field with the three angels hovering in front of them. The lines of soldiers cheered their leaders as Poppy and St. John ceremoniously paraded by. As the roars of adulation from the army grew louder, Angelica peeled off to circle behind the waving pair. In cautionary tones, she whispered to them the traditional words from the days of ancient Rome: "Remember, you are mortal."

Angelica then drew on the magical presence of the goddess, Mother Nature. She ran a powerful piece of music by the composer, Respighi, through their inner minds. Images of the triumphal march along the Appian Way, which the music invoked, burst across their imaginations. Poppy and St. John immediately realised the importance of her warning.

It had been the tradition that when legions of the Roman army returned home from victorious conquests abroad, they marched up the Appian Way to enter the city of Rome via the Appian Gate. Paraded along with the conquering army were exotic animals, slaves and treasure plundered from all parts of the known world to be brought home to swell the coffers of the city. The triumphant commanding general headed the procession. Rome's citizens would line its route to chant their admiration and throw flowers in his path. In such situations, it would be quite easy for generals to be afflicted with visions of personal grandeur that led them to almost believe they were gods. To counter these corrupting influences of self-deception, it was customary that a lowly slave rode in the chariot with the general. Whenever it seemed that the god-like feelings of superiority were swelling within him, the lowly slave was there to repeat in his ear: "Remember, you are mortal." Poppy and St. John only needed reminding once.

St. John reached down and fondled the ears of the wagging Violetta. "What did Mother Nature mean about giving us a fivefold gift do you reckon?"

"Search me," said Poppy. "I was just thinking to myself; if only mum and Flos could see us now."

"They can," said an impish voice behind them. The couple spun round but the swift and agile little god Pan was already back in the bushes smiling with satisfaction. The chariot reached the bottom of the meadow amid the roars of the assembled host and as the horses circled, Xanthus turned and said: "Goodbye St. John. Farewell dearest Poppy. Don't forget the invite from our master, Auriga. Please visit us again for a drive across the heavens."

Before the pair could query what he meant, the three angels fluttered down to give them a hug. "And come to visit us on Honeypot Hill as often as you can."

Just then, Mother Nature swept down on Pegasus and called out: "Remember what you were advised earlier? Everything you have is on loan by the grace of the gods. You are Children of the Stars. The only true, priceless possession you have on this Earth, now and hereafter, is that with which you came into this world – the pure light and star energy that burns within your heart and soul."

With that, Pegasus gave one sweep of his wings and shot skywards. As he did so, Mother Nature leaned out, waved her farewell and then swept her arms over them. There was a stunning flash of white light across the field which left the twin brother and sister temporarily blurred in vision and dazed in mind.

CHAPTER 15

THE HOMECOMING

As the sight and senses of Poppy and St. John cleared, they were aware of a hushed silence. Gradually, it began to fill with the buzzing of bees, singing of birds and the gentle summer's breeze rustling the leaves and whispering the lush green grass of the meadow. They could only stare in disbelief around them. Everyone had gone! All that could be seen were the rainbow armies of wild flowers flourishing across the field. Dotted amongst the kaleidoscope of colour proudly grew the grey/blue Forget-me-nots freshly planted by Mother Nature. Nothing stirred, except for the occasional hare that bounded up the hill and a fox that appeared out of the tree line, looked at them haughtily for their intrusion and then turned its brush to snoot off. St. John felt a tugging at his sleeve. He looked down and saw the devoted eyes of Violetta.

It was only then that he noticed the sleeve the dog was tugging at. His eyes shot to Poppy. It was the same with her. They were back in their tattered sweatshirts, dirty jeans and battered trainers again. Poppy broke the moment: "Well, you can't say that our queen was kidding. She told us that everything we have is only on loan from the gods and it seems as if the divine bailiffs have been to repossess!" They burst out laughing until Poppy's eyes suddenly went wide and she clutched at her neck. She sighed in relief – they both had the necklaces that Mother Nature had bestowed upon them. Poppy accidentally touched one of the miniature gold emblems on her chain and instantly Athena's dagger shot into her hand. She quickly touched the emblem again and the dagger disappeared. It was now St. John's turn to show concern and he scrambled in the pockets of his jeans. He too gave a sigh of relief as his fingers located the glazed eye of Stheno and the letter from Cassius, given to him on their visit to the palace of Andromeda.

Poppy nodded towards his feet and queried: "What are you going to do about that?" St. John looked down to see the goatskin bag containing the head of Stheno. He picked it up with revulsion. "We'll have to take it with us for now until we can think of a safe place to hide it. Come on Poppy, time to go home. Heaven knows how long we've been gone!" Poppy looked at him with a curled lip. "Oh, back to normal is it, with one of your corny jokes?" "No. It wasn't meant as a pun," protested St. John. "You know what I mean. I should think Aunt Kay and half the police force has been out searching for us for goodness knows how many days. I bet she's rung dad and all hell's been let loose." They trudged across the meadow, out onto the cart track and wearily wended their way back towards the village of Tevlingorde. Violetta happily padded along behind them. As they passed its meandering driveway, Poppy gazed yearningly at the empty sprawling buildings of her farmhouse.

In the distance, they saw a lone figure leaving the end of the village to hurry up the cart track towards them. It was Aunt Kay. "That's torn it," muttered St. John. "We're in for a right ear-pasting now. You go first. You're a girl – she won't jump on your head as much as she would me." He grabbed Poppy and pushed her in front of him. She shrugged off her brother and accused him of being a rotten coward. He rolled his eyes in disgust. "You've got to be joking! I've just been through blood, bone and bedlam for you – you ungrateful cat!"

By now Aunt Kay had reached them. "Fancy arguing," she said breathlessly. "Today of all days – on your birthday! Your mum always reckoned you started arguing the minute you were both born. I've been looking all over for you. You must have been up early this morning to have your breakfast – you have had your breakfast haven't you? – go out for a stroll and be on the way back before I'd hardly woken up. You should have told me last night that you were going out first thing."

Poppy and St. John looked at each other in amazement. In the vastness of space and the realms of the gods, it seems that the pressured daily bustle of Earth-time meant nothing at all. Time, back home, had virtually stood still.

"Well, come on then," chided Aunt Kay. "Don't stand there. We've got a lot to do. I've had a phone call – well two really. That's what woke me up. Your dad has telephoned. They have let him out of hospital. He's catching the first train down so he can be with you today on your birthday. Isn't that great? Then Professor Poultney rang. He's a lovely man. He's doing a barbecue for you tonight at his house. We've got to take the trifles and cake. Goodness, look at the state of you two. You look as if you've been in a battle!"

Poppy and St. John could not help but smile at her innocent remark. Aunt Kay finally noticed Violetta. "I see you've found a new friend. She's lovely."

"That reminds me, have you seen Pig on your travels? He seems to have disappeared off the face of the Earth." She suddenly stopped chattering and looked closely at Poppy. "There are tears in your eyes. What's the matter?"

St. John stepped in. "Can we go home first Aunt Kay? We need to sit down and talk to you."

Poppy and St. John had already decided that the only way they could explain the disappearance of Pig and the appearance of Violetta was to tell Aunt Kay everything. They knew she was a good person and that they could trust her. Moreover, they would need her support when the time came to explain everything to their dad – especially the White Archangel's little ploy with the poisonous toadstool! They sat at the kitchen table and in between swigging copious amounts of tea and ravenously stuffing crusty

112

bread and strawberry jam, the pair told all. They described everything, from Poppy's dreams on their arrival, the journey to the stars, the gods and goddesses that lived there and the final battle of life and death for the world. Violetta sat with her head in Aunt Kay's lap. Through it all, Aunt Kay's eyes alternately went wide in acknowledgement then narrowed in disbelief at their story. Her stroking of Violetta's head became increasingly vigorous and agitated. As final proof, Poppy touched her gold emblem and Athena's jewel-encrusted dagger shot into her hand. St. John did the same with Athena's sword. He dare not do the same with his emblem of the winged horse, for fear that Gaspeus would fill the cottage kitchen and a sweep of his wings might smash every piece of bone china on Aunt Kay's Welsh dresser. St. John picked up the goatskin bag and said: "For obvious reasons, I can't show you the head of the Gorgon, but I've got it here." Just to see the red stain at the bottom of the bag was enough to convince Aunt Kay. "Lord help us," she moaned. "Go and lock it in the wood shed right now!"

The rest of the morning was taken up with baths, making a bed up for dad and producing a trifle. Each was deep in personal thoughts and keeping busy was a way of helping them accept the magnitude of what had taken place. Occasionally a sigh of disbelief and a mutter of "heaven forbid" from Aunt Kay brought the event back into conversation and they talked the whole thing through again and again.

Each time, this involuntary form of group therapy helped them get to grips with the implications of it all. Gradually it became more readily accepted.

In the afternoon, they jumped into Aunt Kay's battered Land Rover and headed off to the railway station at Market Harborough to collect dad. Violetta sat happily in the open back as though she had been there all her life. There were many hugs, tears and kisses on the station platform with dad before they set off back to the village. This time, the twins sat in the back and Violetta sat in the front on the cowling between Aunt Kay and dad. Aunt Kay subtly tried to drop hints to him of what was to be revealed when they got back to the cottage.

In fact, when it came to the crunch, dad displayed all the attributes of his personality that his kids and their mum had always loved him for. He remained calm, thoughtful and understanding. Apart from a few questions to help him get things clear in his mind he only made one telling comment. His words were enough to reassure Poppy and St. John of his utter support and belief in them. Gently, he pulled them onto his knee, gave them a hug and said: "I fell in love with your mother and have never stopped loving her since because she was a very special person. Why should I be amazed, or surprised, that her children are special too?"

CHAPTER 16
A Night to Remember

That evening they all walked down the cart track and turned up the driveway to Professor Poultney's house. As they walked up the path, dad noticed Poppy dawdling and looking behind her. The moonlight lit their track, but it also lit the other track that led to her farmhouse. "It's alright," laughed Aunt Kay. "Poppy is wishing again about owning that empty farm up there. I've already told her it would take a chest full of gold to buy it but if you can't have daydreams when you're young it would be a sorry world."

Professor Poultney provided a terrific barbecue and to top the evening gave them each a birthday present. For Poppy, he presented a professional artist's watercolour and oils kit contained in a beautiful wooden carrying case. He already had a watercolour painting of wild flowers that she had given him. It hung in pride of place over his mantle piece. "I have given you this because you have a real talent for painting wild flowers," he said. "If only he knew the half of it," whispered dad in Aunt Kay's ear. Then he presented St. John with a gift that he could only dream about. It was a state-of-the-art telescope. "I thought this would be a very apt gift because I want to encourage you to keep on with your astronomy," he urged. "For a young person, you seem to have such an in-depth knowledge of the stars." Aunt Kay shot a glance at their dad. He winked back at her.

St. John and Poppy carried the telescope down to the bottom of the lawn and set it up near the summerhouse. Immediately, he trained it on the constellation of Canis Major, the 'Great dog'. "Can you see him?" asked Poppy urgently. "Yes. Yes. There he is!" replied St. John in triumph. "The star is too small and faint to see with the naked eye but it is plain as day with this super instrument." Poppy pushed him aside to have a look at the immortalised Pig. By now, the adults had strolled down to join them. "You pair seem rather excited. What have you seen?" queried Professor Poultney. "We've found a new star," declared Poppy with pride. They stood back to let him have a look. "This is unbelievable," he gasped, as he looked then looked again. "You do realise that as the discoverers of a new heavenly body, you have the sole right to name it. Most discoverers name it after themselves and make their mark in astronomical history. Is that what you wish to do?" "No," said St. John without hesitation. "We wish to name it Porcus." Professor Poultney scratched his head in puzzlement, while Aunt Kay asked what it meant. Poppy hugged her and whispered in her ear: "It is the Latin word for Pig. We told you what Athena and Mother Nature said they would do and they have kept their promise to us." They clung to each other and shed a tear for their beloved friend.

A little later in the evening, while Aunt Kay sat on the patio with a glass of wine chatting about the exciting star discovery with Professor Poultney, dad and the twins slipped away to sit in the summerhouse. They had been apart for a while and needed time to themselves to catch up on family matters. As today was the twins' birthday, it was only natural that dad started to reminisce about the day they were born. He remembered the morning when mum had suddenly gone into labour. Dad had been working on night shift so he was in bed. He jumped up, got dressed in a panic and biked down the street to the telephone box to call an ambulance. When they got to the hospital, he found that he was wearing one slipper, one brown shoe and his shirt tail was hanging out at the front – snagged in the zip of his trousers. He could not get the zip to move and had a right game in the 'Gents' doing a sort of Samba dance in the cubicle, trying to force his trousers over his hips so he could go to the loo! They all laughed and it started them off talking about the good times they had with mum. The tears welled up in dad's eyes. It was the first time Poppy had seen him cry since mum's death. She guessed that he had kept it bottled up inside to keep strong for his children.

"The letter!" exclaimed St. John. "The letter that Cassius left for us at Andromeda's palace." He pulled it out and read it aloud to them:

If you should survive the ordeals to come,
And the tasks you face are successfully done.
On your pending birthdays – if memories sad,
Of good times with mother you do not now have.
Come flooding your mind, making heart and soul sink,
Look to the night sky – see your blues turn Rose pink.

St. John grabbed their hands. "Come with me. I think I know what Cassius was telling us. Everyone look up to the heavens and keep looking all around." They stood on the lawn, casting their eyes around the sky. "What are we supposed to be looking for?" dad asked him. "That!" shouted St. John excitedly. He pointed across to a dot of white light coming from the direction of the North Star. When it drew nearer to them, they could see the silver light of a comet with a long shimmering tail. As it passed overhead, something wonderful happened. The tail burst into a brilliant pink colour. "This is unbelievable," muttered dad. "It's pink. The tail has turned pink."

Poppy clutched his arm: "No dad. It's not just pink. It is Rose pink. In fact, it is Rose Flos pink! Remember when I told you that we visited the constellation of Ursa Major and I sat and talked to Callisto? She told me that we don't really die. The atomic building blocks that we are made from – forged twelve billion years ago in the first giant stars – just disintegrate then recycle in the magic circle of life to be re-used for a new life. However, the pure light-energy of the stardust that is contained deep within our souls still

117

burns brightly. Once freed from those building blocks, it flies back to our first birth-home amongst the stars in the heavens. We keep our earthly form, but without the troublesome burden of bodily substance. We are pure light-energy again and can leap so fast amongst the stars that we can be almost everywhere at once and anywhere we want to be."

Poppy clutched her dad's arm even tighter then looked into his eyes. "Callisto told me that one day, when this happens to me, I will join mum and we will dance hand in hand amongst the moonbeams, spin with the planets and ride the comets together. That is mum up there, riding the comet – free from pain, free from worry. The universe is her playground. Deep inside, I know that Athena has allowed mum to visit us on our birthdays. Isn't it wonderful?"

Poppy and dad clung to each other and through tears of joy, watched mum's majestic progress across the heavens. St. John reached a hand up to the night sky. It was as though he could touch her and his soul felt the comforting warmth of mum's starlit embrace once again.

The next day, as the morning sunlight filtered through the cottage windows, Poppy awoke to the smell of bacon and freshly baked bread drifting up into her bedroom. She could hear the muffled voices of Aunt Kay, dad and St. John coming from the kitchen. After a long deep sleep, her fuddled mind momentarily thought that the whole previous episode had been a fantastic dream. Then she looked across to the other pillow on the feather mattress bed and saw the soft brown eyes of the curled-up Violetta waiting to greet her. Suddenly, Aunt Kay struck the little brass dinner-gong that hung in the hall and shouted: "Breakfast!" Automatically Poppy brought her knees up and covered her head with her hands, in anticipation of being trampled to death by Pig's determined efforts to be first to the food. The absence of the usual chaos that Pig caused on these occasions and the stark reality of recent events cut through the cotton wool of her sleep-drugged mind. She staggered down to the breakfast table.

Dad took her hand and said: "I was just saying to St. John, we have to go home tomorrow. I have to get back to work otherwise I will lose my job."

Poppy groaned inside. "Back to the grey, concrete estate and the hard-nosed kids," she thought to herself. "Also," continued dad, "Aunt Kay was wondering what you were going to do with that monstrosity in the wood shed." St. John interceded and told them that they intended to bury it but diplomatically pointed out that he and Poppy had to do it alone. The knowledge of its whereabouts could endanger anyone who knew. For the safety and security of everyone, it was best kept solely to the two of them.

Chapter 17

Life Moves in Great Circles

After breakfast, the two fetched the bag that contained Stheno's head and set off together towards Honeypot Hill. St. John hefted a garden spade on his shoulder. They had already decided that this was the best place to hide it. If anyone should get too close to discovering it, they were sure that the ever-watchful White Archangels would somehow get a message up north to warn them. They set off down the cart track. As they passed the track that led up to the empty farmhouse, Poppy saw a car parked in the driveway. Her heart sank. *Her* farm must have been sold, or was surely in the course of being disposed of. She knew it was silly of her to feel so disappointed and despondent. After all, they had enough of a struggle back home to pay the rent on the council house and meet the weekly bills of day to day living. How could she ever afford to buy that? She would have to win the Lottery Jackpot first and the odds against doing that were one in fourteen million! "I'd stand more chance of flying to the Moon," she thought to herself then burst into laughter at the irony of her unintended joke. "Are you alright?" quizzed St. John. She did not reply but fell in behind him to trudge dejectedly in silence. St. John did not press her further, assuming that the strain had finally taken its toll on his sister.

They decided to bury the head at the foot of the hill but well up into the tree line so as to avoid the risk of being accidentally seen doing it by anyone. They came across a Rowan tree, which

120

seemed as good a place as any other. St. John slung the spade off his shoulder, put his foot to it and pressed it into the earth. Before the spade had gone halfway in, he froze. There came the snapping sound of twigs, the noise of something crashing through the bushes and the most fearful echoes that had ever assailed his ears – the clanging of metal. "My God, it can't be," he hissed under his breath. "I buried the body myself!" Poppy gripped his hand: "Stheno's body couldn't live without her head could it? Please tell me it couldn't," she pleaded anxiously. St. John could not tell her a lie. He just did not know for sure. "Perseus told me he slung Medusa's head in the sea straight after he slaughtered her and that was that" he shrugged. "Perhaps we shouldn't have kept Stheno's head 'til now. Her body might have clawed its way out of the grave and has come to look for her head. How the hell do I know? Come on!" He started running up the hill, yanking Poppy behind him. As they veered to the left, the snapping of twigs and clanging of metal came crashing towards them from the left. They veered right but the sound of the Gorgon's corpse switched around and now came hammering towards them again from the right. Each time they changed direction, the sounds of the crashing corpse changed with them. In desperation they ran straight ahead up the hill until their heaving chests could no longer draw sufficient breath to keep their legs moving. They could run no more and slumped with their backs to the lone Yew tree that grew on Honeypot Hill.

Pan smiled to himself. "Thanks very much kids," giggled the little god. "That's just where I want you." He threw away the two horseshoes he had been clanking together. They were no longer needed now. Meanwhile, St. John had accepted they could not escape and decided he would make his stand and fight on this very spot. He fingered the gold emblems on his chain and instantly, the shield and sword of Athena appeared in his hands. Needing both hands free to shift the shield well up onto his forearm for close combat, he leaned to the side to push the sword's tip upright into the ground beside his right thigh. As he did so, he nearly fell over as the sword thrust straight through the earth up to its hilt. A jarring thud ran through the sword and up his arm. Try as he may, he could not get the leverage to free it. Cursing and sweating with panic, he wrenched and heaved at it. Then he heard a movement behind the Yew tree. It was too late. They were dead!

Pan snapped his fingers and brought forth a creation out of thin air that would provide a logical explanation for the twins as to what had just put the fear of death into them. Then he gave his creation a mighty shove and fell about choking with stifled laughter as he heard the wailing words of surprise rise up from St. John's bone-dry mouth: "What the devil......! Who the heck put that......? Where's that come from?" The startled face of a Guernsey cow, with a clanging cowbell around its neck, popped from behind the tree trunk. Poppy and St. John looked at each other and then burst into fits of uncontrollable laughter. It was not so much the humour of the situation that was making them laugh. It tended more towards hysteria born from the sudden release of extreme stress. Pan took advantage of the noise they were making to release his own guffaws as he frolicked around in the grass. He loved to put the wind up people and cause a good Pan-ic.

After the pair had readily assimilated Pan's contrived explanation and regained their composure, they pulled at the sword together. "Go on my beauties," muttered Pan as he secretly watched them with anticipation. "One more good pull and that'll do it." The pair gave one more pull and sure enough, it did do it. The ground at the roots of the Yew tree collapsed and they now stood waist high in the resulting hole! Pan clasped his hands to his mouth to stifle his giggles. "They'll be alright now," he thought to himself. "The great and wonderful god Pan has succeeded again! Justice is done. The great circle of history has been completed."

"Right, oh glorious one, you've done your bit," he said out loud to himself. "It's back to Greece for tea and tarts – and you can interpret that how you like!" Pan sniggered at his own *double entendre*. A small whirlwind of hot air sprang up around him and in a puff of pollen he disappeared.

St. John climbed out of the hole and then dragged Poppy up. On the way, her shoes scraped on something solid at the bottom. "There's something down there," she told him. "It's what the sword must be jammed in. Don't try and pull the sword straight up, just lever it sideways." They hung over the hole and pulled the haft of the sword sideways towards them. The covering of soil slid away and the lid of an iron chest swung open. At the instant the sun's rays filtered through the branches of the Yew tree and caught the chest's contents, the pair also caught their breath. It was full of hundreds and hundreds of solid gold Roman coins. Each one bore the head of the Roman emperor Claudius. The glitter of the gold in the sunshine made their hearts leap. Only one item did not glitter; it was a flat, square shaped case, somewhat similar to a leather wallet, but made of lead. "We need help with this lot," said St. John as he finally released the sword. He touched the emblems on his chain and the sword and shield of Athena disappeared. He rammed the goatskin bag, containing the head of the Gorgon, into a gap by the side of the chest. Then they covered the hole with brushwood.

Without stopping for anything, they ran home to enlist the help of dad and Aunt Kay with her battered but trusty Land Rover. On the way back to the scene, they picked up Professor Poultney. He was a highly educated man and might be able to throw some light on their discovery. With rope and the four-wheel drive, the chest was pulled out of the hole onto the grass. The professor queried the bag but St. John passed it off as some old bones for Violetta that she had turned her nose up at. He quickly covered it up, retrieved the spade and filled the hole in completely. The amount of gold coins turned out to be more than their wildest estimations. They gave up trying to count the contents at the scene and put them all back in the chest.

While they were doing that, Professor Poultney became intrigued with the lead wallet. Gently, he prised it open with his penknife. Inside was a clay tablet inscribed with Latin text. His Latin was a bit rusty but he managed to carefully pick his way through the words with increasing amazement. Aunt Kay looked over his shoulder in curiosity to ask what it meant. He looked at her seriously and said: "Normally I would say we simply don't know but from the scant personal knowledge that I have of those two young people over there, the meaning has fantastic implications. Tell me Kay, is it right what they told me once – their middle names are Flos and Cassius."

"Yes" she replied. "It's been a family tradition since time immemorial. Why?"

"And that ring that Poppy wears?" he continued.

"Oh, yes. The one with the 'A' and unusual diamond pattern on it," replied Aunt Kay, who was now becoming intrigued by his questions. "It's been passed down through the female line for untold generations. Poppy told me yesterday that she has now found out that it belonged to an immortal named Andromeda."

At her last sentence, the professor's eyes went wide. "I think you should bring them over here to listen to this," he urged.

They all gathered around him but before he started reading the text aloud, he took Poppy's hand and studied the ring closely. He was a world famous astronomer so what he saw confirmed his suspicions. The diamonds represented the exact pattern of stars in the constellation of Andromeda. He looked at Poppy incredulously, gave a nervous cough and then began to read:

'This is the sole property of we, the undersigned. In the event of our death, we bequeath it to our son, Paulus Cassius, and our daughter, Andromeda Flos. In the event that they are prevented from claiming it, then it shall become the sole property of their heirs and descendants – whoever they may be. They shall be recognised by two forms of identification: The males shall always bear the name of Cassius and the females shall bear the name of Flos. Additionally, the female will wear a distinctive ring. It is the Ring of Friendship, which was given by the glorious goddess, Athena, in gratitude to the selfless Princess Andromeda, whom

she later made immortal in the stars. In turn, Andromeda gifted it to me – as a symbol of our eternal friendship. I have since passed it to my daughter, Andromeda Flos, upon her marriage. That is what is and forever more it be. You shall know the rightful owners of this inheritance by these things.

Signed: Flos & Cassius.

Everyone stood looking at St. John and Poppy in awe. It was dad who broke the stunned silence. He put his arms around them and said: "Well, your ancestors might be two thousand years late but you can't say they didn't make up for it with a fantastic birthday present! It must be worth millions." They transported it back to Aunt Kay's cottage and it was decided that Professor Poultney should ring the Ancient History and Archaeology Department at the University of Leicester to seek their expertise.

While the adults were busying themselves on the telephone and going through the treasure chest, Poppy slipped quietly out of the front door. She had gone no more than a few paces down the lane when a voice from behind said: "I know where you're going. I'll come with you for support." She smiled at her brother's intuitiveness.

Chapter 18

Life Moves in Small Circles

They walked down to the empty farmhouse together. The car was still parked in the drive. St. John stood close behind her as Poppy took a deep breath and rapped the brass fox-head doorknocker. The oak wood door swung slowly open. A portly woman confronted the pair with a round-faced smile.

"Are you still the original owner, or are you the new owner?" queried Poppy with bated breath. She closed her eyes, dreading an answer she did not want to hear. The woman's reply did not clarify her questions. "Bless you my dear. If only I was either. I'm the cleaner. Hold on, I'll go and fetch him." She half closed the door and went off. Poppy could hear distant muffled voices down the hallway. The suspense of waiting was killing her. The door opened again and the cleaning lady gave her another big round smile. "I can't find him. He was about somewhere earlier though." Poppy's heart sank. "But," continued the woman, "his son and daughter are coming. Hang on a minute." The door half closed again to leave the pair anxiously shuffling their feet on the broad stone steps.

More sounds of footsteps came along the polished oak floor of the hall and the front door opened wide. Starbursts of elation sparkled all around as four pairs of surprised eyes gazed at each other in bewilderment. Once more, St. John was diving with abandon into the deep pools that were Fran's eyes and a surge of desire welled in Tony's at the vision that was Poppy. After clinging hugs, Tony and Fran led the pair into the drawing room and sat them down. There was so much to talk about they hardly knew where to begin. Yes, the security people had given them a good grilling, but Tony and Fran had stuck to the story that they had seen nothing. As far as they were concerned, their survival was due to a well-designed aircraft and the fact that miracles can actually happen. At least the last bit was literally true anyway! Questions from Tony and Fran about the Golden Arrow of Abaris were unavoidable. Poppy and St. John managed to give them a watered-down story of how they came to be on the arrow. It was just enough to explain away the events of that night but even this highly censored story left Tony and Fran dumbfounded at its telling.

It was then that their father, John, walked into the room. He was just as pleasantly shocked at the coincidence of their meeting again as his children had been. Fran could not wait to relate the story she had just been told of the Golden Arrow to her father. He sat down and listened with fascination, occasionally looking at St. John who nodded the purported correctness of the story his daughter was relating to him. He also noticed that Fran was squeezing St. John's hand rather tightly as she babbled on. Cunningly seizing the opportunity to leave the room, Tony offered to make some tea. He quickly grabbed Poppy's hand and took her with him. A little later, they returned with a tray of tea and biscuits. Both looked flushed in the face from the excitement of taking a moment to snatch a long kiss. However, Poppy's face was a little more flushed than Tony's, having discovered that his dad owned the farm. What is more, he had not sold it but was thinking of doing so. That is why they were at the farmhouse – to start clearing out the personal items of their deceased grandparents.

They all sat down again. By now, Fran had finished retelling the twins' fantastic tale and John was still left uncertain as to how to make sense of it all. One thing he was certain of though, that these mysterious young people had saved the life of himself and his children. It was then that he enquired as to why Poppy and St. John came to be at the farmhouse now. St. John explained how they had accidentally discovered the treasure chest and how it was proved beyond doubt that it had belonged to their ancestors and now subsequently belonged to them. "And that," said Poppy, "is why we are here. We have the means to buy the farm and its land."

"Well, you'll certainly have plenty of land," replied John, "because it stretches for miles down the cart track, up to and including the massive meadowland at the bottom. What is more, it includes Honeypot Hill, though what use you could have for that, or any of it, I can't imagine."

Poppy explained her reasons with zeal. In conclusion, at the end of outlining her project, she informed him that she already had plans where to get the team of builders from and the personnel to staff the estate. John was impressed. "Look," he said. "I have contacts in the Department for Overseas Aid and Development. What's more, I also have a lot of contacts abroad in the developing countries. I could help you with arrangements on the transport and political side if you want."

"Does that mean you will sell it to us?" asked Poppy excitedly. He smiled: "I couldn't think of selling it to two better people, or for a better reason." He stuck out his hand and they shook. Poppy and St. John took the Travis family back to introduce them to dad and Aunt Kay and the final sequence of events evolved from there.

The twins returned home up north and packed their possessions to move into the farmhouse. The day before they exchanged their inner-city home for the rural village of Tevlingorde, dad took the twins into the estate's community college to explain that he would be transferring them to finish the last couple of terms of their schooling in the Midlands. While he was doing that, the pair went off to say goodbye to their favourite teachers. On the way, the school bully, Big Gob-Lin, and her gang of pixies ambushed Poppy in reception. They pinned her in the corner next to a large decorative palm plant and threatened to "do the snobby little cow over". As Big Gob-Lin yanked at Poppy's hair, the palm plant spun round in its pot and one of its stiff, jagged, broad leaves gave her such a smack in the kisser that you wouldn't believe! It made her cry with the pain. Her gang just stood there, horrified at the bright red welt across their gang leader's face. While they fussed around the blubbering bag of wind, Poppy calmly walked away. As she did so, she whispered over her shoulder: "Thank you for your kind help." Back came the reply from the palm plant: "No problem Princess."

A caretaker, passing by the office, commented to the secretary: "Is that girl talking to herself?" "Oh Poppy?" replied the woman. "Yes, there's always been something strange about her."

The gang of bully boys that had plagued him for years waylaid St. John in a corridor. He was pushed against the wall and their leader demanded to know what was in the little bag tied around St. John's neck. If it was any good then they would have it. Keeping his gaze straight ahead, St. John loosened the bag to comply with their demands for a quick flash of the contents. A glimpse of Stheno's eye was enough to freeze the lot of them to the spot. St. John took a black marker pen from the boy's pocket, wrote "the principal is a fat fart' in giant letters across the newly-painted walls, stuck the pen in the frozen leader's outstretched hand and walked off. In the distance he could hear the shouts of the deputy head as he discovered the new graffiti and the babbling of the bullies, now rudely awakened from their stupor by a tirade from the furious principal.

CHAPTER 19
POPPY'S PLAN

The family returned to Tevlingorde. Aunt Kay was waiting at the railway station for them. It was good to be back and the reunion was a happy occasion. The only thing that marred it was the absence of Violetta. She had gone missing shortly after Poppy and St. John had left with dad to tidy up affairs in the north. Aunt Kay had looked for her everywhere without success. The twins were also unsuccessful in their searches for her and could only assume that she had grown home-sick and returned to Honeypot Hill.

Once they had settled in the farmhouse, Poppy set about fulfilling the dream project that she had outlined to John Travis. It was her intention to create a haven for suffering children of any nationality, like the one at Andromeda's heavenly palace, only here on Earth. To do that, she would need builders to convert the barns into dormitories, build playrooms and above all, create an extensive kitchen and dining area. Poppy's long-term requirement was for cleaners to maintain the premises, staff for the kitchens and most importantly, carers for the children that would be sent to stay from far and wide. Moreover, she wanted to stock the farm with animals and grow farm produce, so that the project would be as self-sufficient as possible. For this, she would require farm workers to take care of those things.

Poppy went back with St. John to Honeypot Hill. There, the 'Princess of Wild Flowers' knelt down among her selected plants and talked to them. This bit of magic ritual was beyond St. John's understanding, so he took the opportunity to sit under the Yew tree and daydream of Fran. The wild flowers that Poppy approached had volunteered without hesitation to her request for help. She passed her hands over them and said: "By the power given to me on my crowning day, you wild flowers will become the things that I say."

The common British wild flowers, specially selected by reason of their names, quivered and shook, then transformed into the personnel that Poppy desired.

'Stonecrops' became stone masons and brick builders. 'Cleavers' became hewers of wood and carpenters. 'Welds' became steel erectors, plumbers and electricians. The skills of the workers, magically instilled by each flower's name, would convert, refurbish and construct new buildings at Poppy's sanctuary for suffering children.

'Lady's Smock' arose from the earth as white-smocked kitchen staff and 'Broom' became the cleaners and maintenance staff.

For the care and nurture of the children, Poppy selected two wild flowers: 'Medicks' were transformed into nurses and 'Heartsease' became dormitory housemothers.

To stock her farm, Poppy selected 'Pignuts' for pigs, 'Cowslips' for her milking herds, 'Sheep's Scabious' for flocks of sheep and 'Chickweed' became broods of hens to provide fresh eggs.

'Ploughman's Spikenard' turned into farm workers to plough the fields and tend the animals.

As a special creation, Poppy transformed the 'Coltsfoot' once again but this time not into the huge shire horses that carried her knights into battle. Now they were turned into ponies for the children to ride for fun.

Poppy and St. John gathered them all together and made ready to lead them down to the farm. As they started to move off, there was a flash of white light and a cloud of self-raising flour showered over the pair. They could only stand and stare in amazement. Plonked on a tree stump, with a rolling pin in her hand, sat the roly-poly Lares from Andromeda's kitchens. "Ah! There you are my dears – got the right place at last," she blustered. "I've had a right journey don't you know? Just accidentally gate-crashed some T.V. studio when I hit Earth, with some man prancing up and down pretending to give a cookery demonstration. The stuff was all fancy muck! And as for his dumplings – the best thing he could have done with them was give them to Lord Nelson for cannonballs and I told him straight, so I did. Believe me, my dears, I know what I'm talking about. He just stood there and stared at me like a ruddy fowl."

St. John was the first to recover from the shock: "Dear Lares, what are you doing here?"

"Well, mistress Andromeda owed me about ninety years in annual leave, so I put in a request for a holiday on Earth. I've decided I might as well spend it as a working holiday and come and look after you pair." She poked St. John in the stomach with her rolling pin. "You've not been eating enough my lad. What you need is a few more treacle puddings!" Then she waved her rolling pin at the workmen. "Anyway, that lot will need feeding won't they?" Then she glared at the kitchen staff: "And if you think that motley collection is capable of doing it – you're wrong! They need a bit of supervision, that's what they need." She rolled up the sleeves of her blouse, looked at Poppy quizzically and said: "Well, come on girl, lead the way!"

Before Poppy left Honeypot Hill, she went to the place where the White Archangels grew and enquired of Angelica regarding the whereabouts of Violetta. Angelica reassured her that Violetta was safe and had gone on a personal quest but would return to the farm when she was ready. Content with that knowledge, Poppy led her workers back to the farm and progress commenced on converting it into a safe haven.

CHAPTER 20
THIS TAKES THE BISCUIT!

One day, Poppy and St. John sat with dad and Aunt Kay in the farmhouse kitchen amid the mayhem of sawing, hammering and dust. As they took a well-earned rest and a cup of tea, the kitchen door was pushed open. "Oh, no," thought St. John, "more complaints and problems from the Lares." Then a head poked around the door and a big pair of smiling brown eyes blinked at them. It was Violetta. She pushed the door open a little more and trotting through her front legs wobbled three cuddly golden Labrador puppies. Ecstasy followed as the family hugged Violetta and rolled around on the floor playing with her three new daughters. The joyous moment was broken by Violetta becoming agitated and scratching to get back through the door. "Whatever is the matter Violetta?" asked Aunt Kay. Poppy opened the door that led back to the pantry storeroom and looked around but could see nothing. She was about to turn away when the movement of a cupboard door caught her eye. She pulled it open and looking up at her was another puppy. The little black miniature of Pig stared at Poppy quizzically as if to say "what are you looking at?" and then turned his back on her and continued his efforts to rip open a packet of ginger biscuits. For, as is the way of nature, in the midst of death, there is the rebirth of life.

After several months of hard work and preparation the holiday farm was ready. Dad had taken on the job of premises and estate manager. Aunt Kay, being a qualified chartered accountant, took on the job of finance manager of the fortune that the treasure chest had brought in. John took up the role he had promised of liaison between various governments and aid agencies and made transport arrangements for the needy children to come and stay for long periods of respite. Tony and Fran had spent every weekend at the farm mucking in with the cleaning and now they were going to devote their time to helping care for the children alongside Poppy and St. John. Their relationships blossomed and went from strength to strength. Come to that, Tony and Fran had noted, with a nudge and a wink, their increasingly smiling father seemed to be finding untold excuses for spending time with Aunt Kay.

On grand opening day, they all stood together at the entrance to the farm track, waiting to greet the arrival of the first group of children. As the coach swung into the driveway, it passed under a sign that read:

'The Andromeda – Flos Haven For Little Stars'.

That evening, they all sat around the table in the dining room of the farmhouse and discussed the satisfying events of the first day. Through the open window, drifting on the warm breeze of a new spring, Poppy heard the laughter of children and the soothing words of a housemother from one of the dormitories. Across from the kitchens she heard the rattle of saucepans and the rebuking voice of the huffing Lares. She reached across and squeezed Tony's hand. "Yes," she thought. "Life is good".

THE END

"Hey! Over here! No. Not there! Here. Over the page!"

"Ah. There you are. It's me – the great god Pan. 'What are you doing here?' you may ask. Well, now that the author – who thinks he wrote this trilogy – has gone to make a cup of tea, I'll tell you. Don't get me wrong, he's not totally thick, but he shouldn't have put 'THE END' where he did. I kept telling his subconscious but his little bean-brain refused to take it in. Hang on! Don't tell me you think *he* wrote it all? By the heads of the Hydra! How gullible can you be? Okay, so he did a bit but where do you think he got all the juicy gossip from about the gods and goddesses? Most of his time at the keyboard was spent staring out the window! It's me that put the actual events in his mind and guided his fingers to type the words. He put 'THE END' where he did because he is a bit of a romanticist. His tiny mind overruled my huge superior one and he ended it with a nicey, nicey, happy-ever-after finish. Well, now he's gone out the room, I'll type in the true ending! You know that saying 'nothing is as bad as you think it will be and nothing is as good as you want it to be?' Well, that's what happened here. I hereby write the following true 'THE END':

Poppy reached across and squeezed Tony's hand. "Yes," she thought. "Life is good." It was 9 p.m. and John Travis switched on the television to catch up with the latest international news. The newsreader reported:

"News has just come in of an explosion on board an oilrig in the North Sea. It is understood that no one has been injured and all personnel have been safely evacuated. Engineers reported a blow-back from the drilling equipment prior to the explosion, which sent the drill-bit hurtling hundreds of feet into the air. It is thought that some unknown hazard, deep under the sea bed, may have been disturbed by the drill, which rammed it back up to the ocean's surface."

Poppy dropped the biscuit plate in her lap and St. John spilt his cup of tea all over the table. They sat rigidly staring wide-eyed at each other – as if they had been turned to stone.

"Whatever's the matter?" asked Aunt Kay.

In unison, they muttered one word: "Euryale."

Paul Hayward

"You'd forgotten about her hadn't you? Well, so had they!"
Signed: *Pan* (co-author).

A Bunch of Wild Flowers

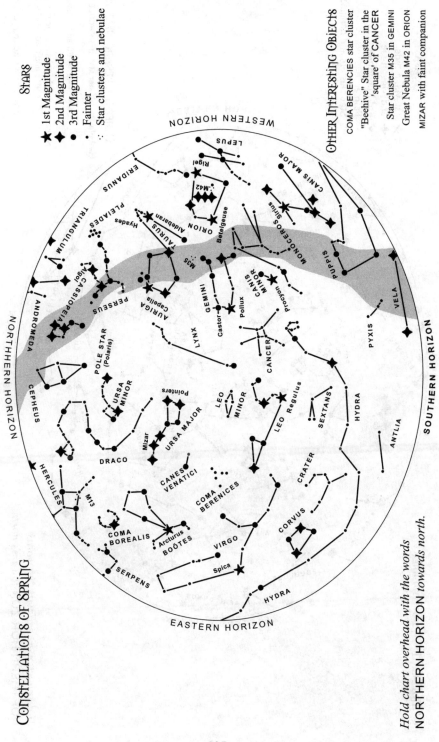

Constellations of Spring

Stars

★ 1st Magnitude
✦ 2nd Magnitude
● 3rd Magnitude
· Fainter
∴ Star clusters and nebulae

Other Interesting Objects

COMA BERENCIES star cluster
"Beehive" Star cluster in the 'square' of CANCER
Star cluster M35 in GEMINI
Great Nebula M42 in ORION
MIZAR with faint companion

Hold chart overhead with the words
NORTHERN HORIZON *towards north.*

137

Paul Hayward

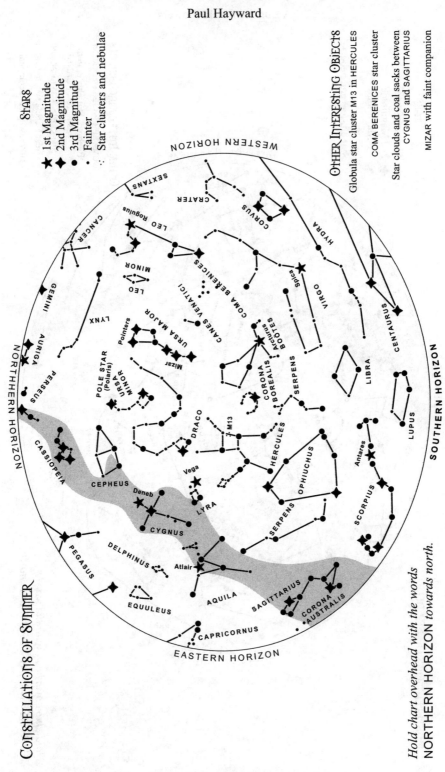

Stars

★ 1st Magnitude
✦ 2nd Magnitude
● ● 3rd Magnitude
· · Fainter
∴ Star clusters and nebulae

Other Interesting Objects

Globula star cluster M13 in HERCULES

COMA BERENICES star cluster

Star clouds and coal sacks between CYGNUS and SAGITTARIUS

MIZAR with faint companion

Constellations of Summer

Hold chart overhead with the words
NORTHERN HORIZON *towards north.*

Constellations of Autumn

Stars

★ 1st Magnitude
✦ 2nd Magnitude
● 3rd Magnitude
• Fainter
⋰ Star clusters and nebulae

Other Interesting Objects

Great Spiral Nebula M31 in ANDROMEDA

Star clouds and coal sacks in Milky Way between CYGNUS and SAGITTARIUS

Globular star cluster M13 in HERCULES

Double star cluster between PERSEUS and CASSIOPEIA

Hold chart overhead with the words
NORTHERN HORIZON *towards north.*

WESTERN HORIZON

NORTHHERN HORIZON

SOUTHERN HORIZON

EASTERN HORIZON

OPHIUCHUS
SERPENS
SERPENS
SAGITTARIUS
CORONA AUSTRALIS
BOOTES
URSA MAJOR
CORONA BOREALIS
M13
HERCULES
LYRA
Vega
DRACO
SAGITTA
CYGNUS
AQUILA
Altair
CAPRICORNUS
MICROSCOPIUM
Mizar
URSA MINOR
Deneb
DELPHINUS
EQUULEUS
Pointers
POLE STAR (Polaris)
CEPHEUS
LYNX
PERSEUS
CASSIOPEIA
Double Cluster
M31
ANDROMEDA
PEGASUS
AQUARIUS
PISCIS AUSTRINUS
Capella
Algol
Fomalhaut
GRUS
AURIGA
TRIANGULUM
ARIES
PISCES
SCULPTOR
PLEIADES
TAURUS
CETUS

Constellations of Winter

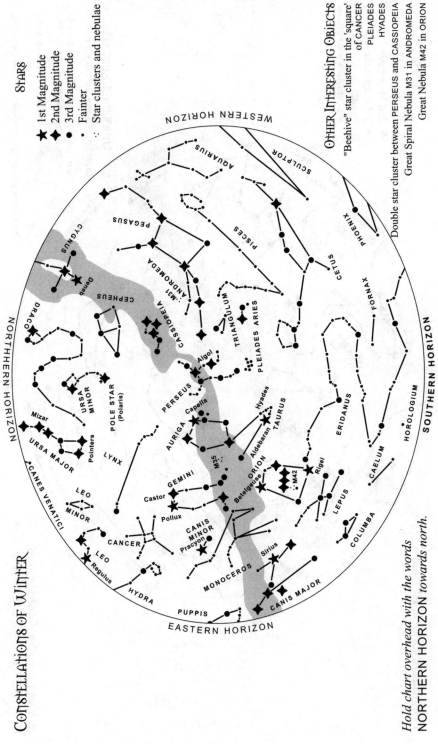

Stars

★ 1st Magnitude
✦ 2nd Magnitude
● 3rd Magnitude
· Fainter
∴ Star clusters and nebulae

Other Interesting Objects

"Beehive" star cluster in the 'square' of CANCER
PLEIADES
HYADES

Double star cluster between PERSEUS and CASSIOPEIA
Great Spiral Nebula M31 in ANDROMEDA
Great Nebula M42 in ORION

Hold chart overhead with the words
NORTHERN HORIZON *towards north.*

 Useful Contacts

For further information about the Wildflower Trilogy and its author, Paul Hayward, visit:
www.the-wild-flower-trilogy.com

For further information about astronomy you can contact:
National Space Centre
Exploration Drive
Leicester
LE4 5NS
Telephone: 0166 261 0261
Email: info@spacecentre.co.uk
Web: www.spacecentre.co.uk

For further information about British wild flowers you can contact:
Plantlife International
14 Rollestone Street
Salisbury
Wiltshire
SP1 1DX
Telephone: +44 (0) 1722 342730
Fax: +44 (0) 1722 329035
Email: enquiries@plantlife.org.uk
Web: www.plantlife.org.uk

ChildLine
ChildLine is the UK's free 24-hour helpline for children and young people in danger or distress, who can call ChildLine on 0800 1111 for help with bullying, abuse or any other problem.